"I'm going to get the last l...

The jester brought up a large butcher knife, the blade glinting under the pale light.

Teegan screamed and grabbed his forearm, trying to hold off the sharp blade, but he was strong. Unimaginably strong for her petite strength to match. A crack of gunfire erupted, giving the jester pause. Another shot fired and Rhode hollered her name.

The jester jumped to his feet and pointed the knife at her. "This isn't over." He hurled an insult and darted into the darkness.

Where he belonged.

Teegan sprang to her feet, her stomach in a tangle of knots as she darted toward the sound of Rhode's voice. She ran straight into him and shrieked.

"It's okay. It's me. You're safe." Rhode cupped her face. "The babies are safe. Did he hurt you again?"

Teegan rubbed her head where it had smacked the solid earth as she fell. "No. He came out of nowhere. How did he know we were here?"

Rhode released a long, heavy breath. "He's watching, Teegan. He's watching."

Jessica R. Patch lives in the Mid-South, where she pens inspirational contemporary romance and romantic suspense novels. When she's not hunched over her laptop or going on adventurous trips with willing friends in the name of research, you can find her watching way too much Netflix with her family and collecting recipes for amazing dishes she'll probably never cook. To learn more about Jessica, please visit her at jessicarpatch.com.

Books by Jessica R. Patch

Love Inspired Suspense

Texas Crime Scene Cleaners

Crime Scene Conspiracy
Cold Case Target
Deadly Christmas Inheritance

Quantico Profilers

Texas Cold Case Threat
Cold Case Killer Profile
Texas Smoke Screen

Cold Case Investigators

Cold Case Takedown
Cold Case Double Cross
Yuletide Cold Case Cover-Up

Love Inspired Trade

Her Darkest Secret
A Cry in the Dark
The Garden Girls

Visit the Author Profile page
at LoveInspired.com for more titles.

Deadly Christmas Inheritance

JESSICA R. PATCH

LOVE INSPIRED SUSPENSE

INSPIRATIONAL ROMANCE

LOVE INSPIRED® SUSPENSE
INSPIRATIONAL ROMANCE

Recycling programs
for this product may
not exist in your area.

ISBN-13: 978-1-335-48394-2

Deadly Christmas Inheritance

Love Inspired
22 Adelaide St. West, 41st Floor
Toronto, Ontario M5H 4E3, Canada
www.LoveInspired.com

Printed in U.S.A.

The Lord is merciful and gracious, slow to anger,
and plenteous in mercy. He will not always chide:
neither will he keep his anger for ever.
He hath not dealt with us after our sins;
nor rewarded us according to our iniquities.
—*Psalm* 103:8–10

To my nephew, Taylor. You probably think
I've run through the whole family and you're the only
one left for a dedication. I mean, you're not wrong.
But maybe I'm just saving the best for last. *Wink. Wink.*

To the host of people who make these books work!
Susan L. Tuttle, Jodie Bailey, Shana Asaro, the team
at Harlequin, Rachel Kent and my husband, Tim.
I couldn't do this without any of you!

ONE

The Landoon mansion loomed over the grassy knoll, boasting its grandeur and alluding to hidden secrets.

Teegan Albright, Lorna Landoon's next-to-newest employee and her full-time caregiver for the past six months, approached her fairly new home. As she rounded the curving drive, she bypassed the side road that branched toward the stables. A sleek black SUV whizzed by, the driver glaring in her direction.

Charlie Landoon.

Lorna's spoiled-rotten great-grandson. Privileged, wealthy and attractive. He exuded total letchy vibes. Teegan wasn't sorry she'd missed him. Though he rarely visited the main house. That might mean speaking with his great-grandmother, and all Charlie cared about was the winning racehorses he bred on her estate.

After leaving Hollywood in the late '70s, Lorna had returned to her home state of Texas, where she'd established a well-known stable that bred thoroughbreds. Over the years, fifteen of her champion lines had won the Kentucky Derby, earning her a second fortune that could rival Katharine Hepburn's acting career. They had been good friends. And Teegan would know. Her love for the classics filled her with all sorts of trivia about the golden age of Hollywood and it's why she enjoyed and appreciated all of Lorna's stories about film, filmmaking and acting. Teegan had even done some theater—her passion. She adored local theaters, but these past two years she hadn't had much spare time.

Now, Teegan parked behind a beat-up red Jeep. Who did that belong to? No one in Lorna's family.

She glanced at the grand double doors decorated with large holly wreaths and classy red bows. Bloated clouds signaled storms rolling into the Texas Hill Country. Christmas was only one week away, and it might take her that long to wrap all the presents. She jumped out of the car and headed for the trunk. The eight-tiered fountain with a lion head bubbled, and silk poinsettia blooms floated along the largest pool on the bottom.

They decked the house out—even the white horse fencing had wreaths with red bows, and that was a lot of horse fencing. Teegan was thankful she wasn't in charge of the holiday decor. Lorna's newish estate manager, Olivia Wheaton, had made that happen. Teegan had helped Olivia get the job since they'd been close friends in high school.

The only thing Lorna wanted to be kept for family was trimming the tree—a tradition done on Christmas Eve after a festive dinner, though often they bailed, according to Lorna, but she kept it going regardless. Teegan had put her private tree up the day after Thanksgiving. That was her new tradition—one she'd established after her fraternal twins had been born.

She popped the car's trunk and winced. She might have gone overboard on gifts. River and Brook would turn two in January. Probably wouldn't even remember the holiday this far back, but...

Growing up, she and her identical twin, Misty, had had little. When Dad couldn't handle Mom's drinking anymore, he'd left them. They'd been seven. Their mother had surprised them that year by simply remembering it was Christmas. Most years, Teegan and Misty had been on their own for the holidays. Once they'd turned fourteen, they'd walked to the Goodwill and purchased a banged-up tree, missing several lights, and brought it home to decorate using popcorn and coloring pages. On Christmas Day, they'd given each other gifts they could afford from babysitting.

Misty had given Teegan a megaphone for when she directed local plays someday—which she'd done a few times. *Little Women. Our Town. A Christmas Carol.*

She'd loved every single second of it, especially helping teenagers who needed a place to belong. Theater provided community for children who had no one—like herself when she'd been that age. She'd thrust herself into movies, Lorna's movies at the top, and joined a local theater where she'd been loved and valued. The costume director, Mrs. Salvatore, had taken her to church on Sundays, and she'd found a place to belong there, too, in God's family.

But at home…it wasn't warm and welcoming. Some Christmases, Mom had never even left the bedroom unless it was to find another bottle of wine. Teegan's children would never know that kind of life. They would know stability, consistency and, while she may not ever make it rich, they'd know unconditional love and that their mom was sober.

God had truly blessed Teegan—which never went without feelings of awe and reverence. She didn't deserve the kind of love God had lavished upon her. Lorna had not only given her a good-paying job, but had offered her the entire east wing of the main house as her and the twins' living quarters, without docking her check for rent. God's grace was often unexpected—though maybe it shouldn't be. Maybe she *should* expect it since it's who He was—gracious.

But her past wasn't clean.

She didn't deserve such grace and mercy. Yet it had absolutely been God's mercy carrying her through the hardest and darkest of times. Looking back, Teegan had almost bypassed filling out the application to be Lorna's caregiver. Nursing school hadn't been required, and it was one of her favorite actresses. She hadn't expected to be hired, especially having two rowdy twin babies. What ninety-two-year old woman wanted to be saddled with that every day? Granted, Lorna was spry for her age and her mind was sharp.

As it happened, Lorna was the mom, grandmother and friend Teegan had desperately needed. A true godsend.

Taking her bags out of the trunk, she looped the handles on her arm until she had no room left. Her phone dinged with a text from Yolanda and she asked Siri to read it.

"'Take your time and pick them up later. They're sleeping like the sweet babies they are. No trouble at all. I love having them.'"

Lies. They were curious little tornadoes that left a disaster in their wake wherever they went, and now that they were walking, that was everywhere. River had figured out how to scale baby gates and Brook liked anything sparkly, which meant pretty much everything in Lorna's mansion.

"Siri, text Yolanda."

"What do you want to say?"

"'Thank you, you big liar. I'll bring you a cookie and a hug.' Send."

Yolanda, a friend from church, had also been a godsend. She had offered to watch the babies so Teegan could shop a few hours and enjoy a peppermint latte without it growing cold. Now she had time to bake a few holiday treats and maybe even enjoy an hour of a good mystery novel or just stare at a wall in silence. She loved her children but she was flat-out exhausted and forgot what a free minute was.

She opened the right front door, bags teetering and clanking on her arms. Lorna really did need to keep her home locked up, but she'd never been one for safety precautions. No guards and no security. Lorna was well aware people had sneaked onto the property hunting for the decades-old rumor of a hidden treasure buried by Lorna herself. What on earth would she have buried and why?

Teegan wasn't buying it. Nothing was hidden on Lorna's property, but that hadn't stopped scads of teenagers—and some adults—from searching; a few times those teenagers had gotten lost in the labyrinth. With shoddy cell service out there, they'd relied on screaming and crying, which had reached Teegan's ears and she'd had to fetch them.

Lorna never prosecuted a single one. It was some kind of fun game. Leave it to the old sadistic lady she loved so much. For all Teegan knew, it was likely Lorna who had begun the rumors simply to be mischievous.

Using her leg, Teegan kicked the door closed behind her, juggling the toys and rolls of gift wrap piled so high she couldn't even see the floor in front of her.

"Lorna, I'm back. You hungry? I'm going to make oatmeal cookies and gingersnaps. You want a cup of tea?" She'd adopted the proper English teatime, and Teegan loved joining Lorna for tea and biscuits—which were really shortbread cookies, but if one had tea with Lorna, they must be called biscuits. They sipped tea, nibbled biscuits, and Teegan hung on all Lorna's stories. Maybe she'd have a few more today. "Lorna?"

She might not have her hearing aids in and, even with them, Lorna's hearing wasn't that great. Teegan was often hoarse from all the hollering, but Lorna didn't go far these days. Kept to the sitting room and her bedroom on the main floor.

Stairs were difficult now and she refused a walker or cane. That kind of pride was going to result in a broken hip, but Lorna never listened. Probably why caregivers cycled through employment like a revolving door.

Dropping the bags on the massive dining room table, an antique piece that sat twenty people, she headed for the sitting room where Lorna often spent her days reading with her huge magnifier or working her arthritic fingers crocheting, though she never finished a project and admitted she was right terrible at it. Still, she said old ladies were supposed to crochet, knit and quilt, and she was going to finish something someday even it was a potholder.

Teegan knew what to expect for Christmas—a half-done potholder.

"Lorna, I'm back and the kids have more toys than any child should. I might have gone into debt." She was kidding, but she also liked to rile Lorna just to hear her mid-Atlantic accent go into a spiel about being a good steward of what God supplied. The accent of course was a fake one—an upper crust dialect old actors and actresses had made up. She sounded like Hepburn, and Teegan liked to mimic it because it was rather beautiful and refined-sounding. Teegan's dialect was what she'd call Texan bumpkin. Nothing cultured about her or her life.

"You hear me, Lorna? Debt. I'm going into debt." She waited for something. Anything.

That's when she noticed the house was quiet.

Too quiet.

Only the pops and creaks in the old settling wood and the crackle of the real fireplace could be heard. Icy fingers walked up her spine, prickling her scalp.

"Lorna," she called weakly, swallowing hard as she inched toward the sitting room, the chill growing colder with each shaky step.

The Jeep. The red one outside. Someone was here at the main house.

A separate drive led to the stables, bypassing the main house. If the driver of that vehicle had business with Harry Doyle, the manager, they'd park out there. Like Charlie. There was even a sign to let drivers know to go around.

As she approached the winding staircase, she halted. Her feet froze to the marble flooring as her heart thudded in her chest.

Blood oozed along the white-and-black-checkered squares like thick cherry juice. Her mouth flew open at the sight of Lorna lying broken at the bottom of the stairs. Her stomach roiled and she pressed a hand to it, as if pressure might keep her from vomiting.

But Lorna wasn't the one producing so much blood.

Lying near her, slashed multiple times, was Misty.

Her twin.

The red Jeep.

A sob erupted from her throat and she knelt, feeling her sister's pulse, but it was clear she was dead. If the multiple slashes through her skin hadn't revealed that, her vacant eyes staring up at her did. Teegan scrambled to Lorna's side, slipping in the blood and shrieking. She felt for a pulse, praying she would find one.

Nothing.

Lorna had gone to be with Jesus.

Teegan stared in a stupor, gazing on her own bloody hands and back at two people she dearly loved. Finally, her senses kicked in and she scrambled to the dining room table where she'd left her cell phone. The bloody soles of her Converse left a trail of prints. As she grabbed her phone, a sudden awareness struck her and she froze again, hand trembling on the phone.

She was not alone.

She forced herself to turn.

A looming figure dressed in jeans, a black hoodie, and wearing some kind of mask—a jester's mask?—stalked toward her, predatory-like, a very large, very bloody butcher knife gripped in his black-gloved hand.

Teegan darted around the dining room table and her shoes slipped against the marble from the red, wet soles. She crashed to the floor, pulling a dining room chair down with her. Unable to regain her footing, she began crawling toward the kitchen.

To the back door.

To freedom.

The jester continued to come for her. Not rushing or running. But slow and methodical, as if he knew he had plenty of time and no one would hear her cries or screams.

TV background noise reached her ears; the newscaster calling for a vicious storm that would bring lashing winds.

Using the kitchen island as an anchor, she pulled herself up to her feet and darted for the door, but the jester gripped her head, ripping hair from her scalp as he yanked her to him.

The sharp tip of the blade cut into her side with a searing burn and she cried out. A copper pot caught her eye and she snatched it from the counter then slung it toward the jester. The pot caught the side of his shoulder and he released his grip, giving her the chance to dart for the door again. She swung it open.

Freedom!

Just as she crossed the threshold, he wrenched her inside the kitchen.

River and Brook's little faces entered her mind.

She had to fight. For them.

Teegan spotted a rolling pin on the bottom of the open stainless-steel island and dropped to her knees. She grabbed it and sprang up. As he brought the knife down, she counterattacked, whacking him upside the head and shifting his mask, which revealed a white male with a dark stubbly chin.

He stumbled and she swung again, and the jester crashed to the floor. Teegan bolted outside as thunder cracked and lightning split the sky, the wind blowing the trees low to the ground in forceful submission.

Harry. She had to get to him. Harry always carried a gun and kept more than one shotgun in his office. The wind fought against her but, hunching forward, she kept running, her legs threatening to buckle underneath her.

Chest heaving and lungs begging for oxygen, she made it to the stable and hollered for Harry.

He was nowhere to be found. He was always out here!

"Somebody help me!" She closed the stable doors, her side burning like wildfire and blood coloring her sweater with a dark stain. She locked the doors from the inside and ran for Harry's office and to the phone. Horses protested her shrieks with neighs, pawing at their stall doors. Blood whooshed in her ears like cotton rubbing against skin.

She grabbed the receiver and dialed 9-1-1. "Help me! Someone is trying to kill me. He's killed Lorna and Misty. Help me!"

"Ma'am, I need you to calm down and tell me—"

"Calm down? I'm about to be butchered!" Tears streamed down her face. "I have babies!"

"Are your babies in the house?" she asked.

Teegan wiped her running nose. "No." She forced herself to settle enough to give the dispatcher information to send the police and an ambulance.

"Stay on the line with me. Cedar Springs PD is on the way."

"Thank you. Thank you." She remained on the line, shaking uncontrollably and wondering who would have wanted to kill Lorna Landoon. And why had Misty been at the house? She hadn't planned a visit. But Misty was known to find trouble. Had trouble followed her here, leaving Lorna a casualty and Teegan an almost-casualty?

Sirens pealed.

Crouching in the office, she continued to listen to the dispatcher and answer her questions, but her mind reeled and she missed what the dispatcher said.

"I hear them," Teegan said. "They're here."

"Stay where you are. They know which stable you're in. You're going to be okay."

That's when she heard the gunshot.

Rhode Spencer pulled up behind his older brothers, Stone and Bridge, at the Landoon mansion. Rain battered his vehicle as thunder rumbled. Rhode wasn't exactly excited to step out into the downpour; instead he gazed up at the old mansion with its Gothic turrets and towers. He and his brothers and friends had sneaked onto the property dozens of times as teenagers hunting for the rumored fortune buried on the estate.

Rhode had always envied the grand home and property with its many amenities such as the Olympic-size swimming pool, hot tub, tennis courts and the labyrinth and English garden. He'd been raised on a modest ranch twenty-five minutes away, and now, in hindsight, he'd have had it no other way. But back then, he'd wanted to live the luxurious life and keep up with his friends like Beau Brighton—Texas royalty. He'd attempted to compete and it had struck him like a venomous snake, saddling him with the poison of debt up to his eyeballs.

So. Much. Debt.

So much stress.

That's when the real drinkin' had begun, holding him hostage. His career as a Cedar Springs' homicide detective had disintegrated, after which he'd spiraled hard. Went on a weekender with tequila and been hauled from the hotel room in Dallas the next day by his brothers. That's the only reason he even remembered that weekend. They'd hauled his sorry sack to a Christian rehab center where he'd sobered up and returned to his faith. Now, his life was much different and he'd been on the straight and narrow almost three years.

Some days went smoothly. Others, his throat ached for the sauce, especially after his twin sister, Sissy, had almost died at the hands of a vicious serial killer eight months ago. But she'd survived and received her happy ending. Now his best friend and business partner, Beau Brighton, was also his brother-in-law.

Two out of four of his siblings were hitched, which left him and his middle brother, Bridge, riding the bachelor train. Tossing the hood of his poncho over his head, he grabbed his gear and jumped out into the downpour. The crime scene had been cleared an hour ago and their card had been given to Miss Landoon's caregiver, who had called Stone at the advice of their cousin, Detective Dom DeMarco, who was working the case.

Rhode raced to the stoop next to his brothers. Bridge removed his hood and raked a hand through his light brown hair. "You think there's treasure here? Because I haven't found it."

"Well, if *you,* a former FBI agent, didn't find it," Rhode quipped with brotherly sarcasm, "I reckon no one can." He slipped into his white hazmat gear, hating the cold rain.

"Shut up," Bridge muttered. "I'm just saying, I've even scuba-dived in that lake. Nothing. I think it's a farce."

Rhode wasn't thinking about the treasure anymore. Not now that he wore the gear necessary to clean up a crime scene. A young woman had been stabbed over seventeen times, and Lorna Landoon had fallen down the stairs to her death.

The caregiver had narrowly escaped and the stable manager had spied the killer, given a warning shot and chased him, but lost him in the woods behind the house.

Said he'd worn a creepy white mask. If it hadn't been for Doyle's showing up at the stables, they'd have more than one location to clean.

"What do you think of this crime? Don't you find it odd that the very day the care-giver's identical twin shows up, she dies?" Rhode asked.

His eldest brother, Stone, set the biohaz-ard containers—their red boxes as glaring as the bloodstains inside would be—beside him. "She here?" Stone asked, ignoring Rhode's question.

"I don't know. Depends on if she parks in the garage or out front. Dom thinks that someone followed the sister from Califor-nia and killed her, but that doesn't explain the Texas bluebonnets left beside her in a pool of blood."

"I don't know," Stone said. "That's not our job anymore. Our job is to deal with the aftermath."

"I know." But that hadn't stopped Stone from inquiring about the murder that had led them to discover their other sister, Paisley, had been murdered, not died by suicide. He didn't bring that up.

"What's the caregiver's name again? In case she is here."

Rhode scratched his stubbly chin. Needed a good shave. "Teegan Albright."

Bridge raked a hand through his damp hair again, and Stone nodded as he zipped up his hazmat suit. Crime scene cleaning was never easy and often tragic and depressing. That was why Stone had started Spencer Aftermath Recovery and Grief Counseling Services after their eldest sister had died. They'd had no idea who was going to clean up the mess. Stone, seeing a need, had left the Texas Rangers, which was about the time Bridge had resigned from the FBI and Rhode had been deep in his drink.

Rhode had left rehab and begun working for the business, but a few months later had also opened up his own business—Second Chances Investigations. The need to solve mysteries and help people find justice wouldn't leave him. Being a private investigator fulfilled that need. He and Beau had been working hard to build a reputable business, though Rhode couldn't afford to leave the aftermath recovery biz. He owed too much money and needed both sources of income to skate by.

Rhode lived in the apartment above his family's garage for free and was as broke as a beggar in downtown Austin. Not exactly the life he envisioned at thirty-five. No wife. No kids. No American dream for him. No one to blame but himself, even though for a time he'd tried blaming anyone and everyone else, including God. But at the end of the day, he'd had to come to terms with the fact that the mess he was in was due to his own sinful choices.

Sissy's blue SUV whipped into the drive. Beau had bought her a new vehicle with hopes of children coming into the picture. Her two Cavalier King Charles spaniels, Lady and Louie, bounded out and raced like greyhounds to the stoop, jumping on his pant legs for ear scratching. Sissy shrieked at the torrential rain and hurried onto the stoop with them.

"I hate the rain!" she said.

"Why are you even here? There's blood inside," Rhode said. Sissy didn't work assignments with blood. She was squeamish. His twin was a licensed counselor and often helped families with grief counseling, her little Cavs being emotional therapy dogs.

"I'm not here for the blood. I'm here to offer grief counseling services to Teegan and any other employees, as well as family members that might want it. Free of charge to Teegan. She's my friend."

"Who knew near fatalities would bring together besties," Rhode teased. Sissy had almost died on this very property a few months ago when a killer had chased her down inside the labyrinth. Beau had rescued her.

"Oh hush. Teegan is great. She's smart and snarky and… I can't imagine losing my twin." Her voice cracked as she held his gaze.

Rhode couldn't imagine life without her

either. It had been hard enough losing Pai all those years ago and then their dad. But he and Sissy shared a special twin bond that was hard to explain to others. Sissy was literally half of him.

He rustled her hair. "Me neither."

The front double doors opened and Teegan Albright emerged. Rhode remembered seeing her when he'd arrived after Sissy had been attacked on the property. Calling Teegan hot would be disrespectful and not even accurate. She was...like sunshine bursting through the clouds. Not so bright you couldn't look on her, but so beautiful you couldn't look away.

Her shiny blond hair was piled on her head and a few strands fell around her heart-shaped face. She smelled like she'd recently showered—probably washing away the blood. He internally winced.

Her blue eyes were watery and rimmed in red, which matched her pert nose. When she looked at him, his insides shifted and that fuzzy feeling returned.

Did he know her other than seeing her at the estate before?

She hadn't grown up in Cedar Springs or gone to school with him. He wouldn't have forgotten her.

"Teegan!" Sissy said and embraced her, the dogs jumping on Teegan's jeans. Teegan cried on Sissy's shoulder.

It shifted Rhode's heart and sent an ache through him as he remembered the agonizing grief when they'd lost Paisley and their father.

Stone stepped up and broke the embrace. He shook Teegan's hand. "I'm sorry for your loss, Miss Albright."

Rhode hung back, unsure why he didn't want to face her, because she definitely drew him. But he wasn't there for anything other than making it look as if a violent death hadn't occurred. And besides, he had nothing to offer a woman presently. He was the poster boy for Loser. Still, something odd niggled at him. Something like… shame.

"Thank you for coming. It's… I can't…"

Teegan sniffed again and shook Bridge's hand. Bridge looked back, his amber eyes boring into Rhode's. Yes, he was being rude, but he couldn't make himself approach. Finally, Bridge said, "This is our other brother, Rhode." He shot Rhode a scowl and Rhode stepped up and shook her hand.

"I am very sorry for your loss, ma'am," he said through cotton.

She studied him and, for a moment, he saw a spark flash in her eyes before they narrowed as if she were trying to place him too. "Thank you. I know I should have left. My friend Yolanda said I could stay with her, but the family will be here any time, I suspect, and I want to be here."

"Understood," Stone said and followed her inside, then Bridge, Sissy and, finally, Rhode entered.

They made their way to the grand staircase. "So, it happened here," Teegan said without looking at the smeared blood. "I was attacked at the dining room table and from there ran to the kitchen where he stabbed me." She pressed her hand to her side. "From there I ran to the stables."

The place was a frenzy of bloody foot- and handprints. Rhode's insides pulsed with fury from his bones to his brain as he envisioned what had transpired. The feelings were intense and fierce...and weird.

"Are you okay?" he blurted. Teegan Albright was absolutely courageous and a fighter. Good for her.

She touched her side again. "I am. The cut was shallow. I've been treated and given antibiotics for possible infection."

"You get a look at him?" he asked.

Stone shot him a glare.

Rhode wasn't a homicide detective anymore and questioning a victim was no longer his job. Unless, of course, she'd hired him as a private detective—which she hadn't. No, his job was to clean up the aftermath. But he couldn't help himself. A protective instinct had kicked in hard and he couldn't fight it. Nor did he want to.

Teegan shuddered. "He wore a jester's mask. Plastic. The kind that has a string around it. It shifted when I hit him with the rolling pin." Her eyes shifted toward the window, but Rhode was sure she wasn't seeing anything other than the frightening moments she'd endured. "He was a white male with a dark, scruffy chin. I saw that. I think his eyes were dark but I'm not sure if it was dark blue or light brown."

"You were so brave," Sissy said as she squeezed her hand.

Rhode agreed. "He say anything?"

This time Bridge passed him a warning eye.

"No."

If Rhode were the detective on the case, he'd call the PD where Misty Albright had lived in California and inquire about other possible attacks by a man in a cheap jester mask. Then he'd run the MO through the Violent Crime Apprehension Program, or VICAP. See if any matches popped.

A jester's mask was particular.

What did it mean? Why that mask?

Why not an easy-to-find, hard-to-trace black ski mask? The disguise clearly held significance. His investigative instincts kicked into high gear, but this wasn't his job or his case. He stepped out the kitchen door Teegan had used to flee the attacker. Blood crusted the doorknob. Outside, on the patio, the rain beat down and Rhode scanned the area. The water had washed away trace evidence. No blood. No footprints.

Back inside, he reentered the foyer area where his brothers conversed in hushed whispers. Teegan and Sissy had disappeared. "What's going on?"

Stone pointed to the gruesome aftermath. "Stabbing is often personal and the number of stabs reveal Misty Albright was murdered in a rage. But Miss Landoon fell down the stairs. Before or after Misty was stabbed to death? And what was she doing upstairs?"

"Thought that wasn't our job?" Rhode asked. "I saw both y'all's glares."

"In front of the victim's family and close friend? No. Between us, speculation is fair game," Stone said.

He was right. Rhode had no business interviewing a survivor.

Stone continued. "Sissy said Lorna lives on the main floor. How did she get up all those stairs?"

"Elevator?" Bridge asked. "I saw it near the kitchen."

Rhode shook his head. "Dom told me the elevator has been broken for a couple of months. He also mentioned that Miss Albright saw Lorna's great-grandson, Charlie Landoon, on her way up the street. He'd passed her, leaving the estate. She assumed he'd been at the stables. Said he rarely visited Lorna, and used the road running alongside the estate, bypassing the home. Dom's going to question him. Might be right now."

Stone grunted. "Well, we'll leave it to Dom."

Nodding, Rhode said, "I just want to get this done and go." His chest continued to squeeze and it felt like the house was closing in on him. Not so much the house…but Teegan's presence.

"What's up with you?" Bridge asked.

"I don't know." He sighed and combed his hair with his fingers, unsure if he would continue to grow it out or chop it. Currently, his bangs hung to his cheekbones and drove him a little batty. "I...think I know the caregiver."

"Know her how?" Stone asked warily.

Heat flamed in Rhode's cheeks. "Like... in the biblical sense."

Bridge huffed and rolled his eyes. "Really? Is there anyone in fifty miles of Cedar Springs you haven't *known*?"

"That's a low blow," Rhode muttered.

"Fitting, don'tcha think?" Bridge asked, sarcasm dripping like acid.

Bridge might be exaggerating, some, but in Rhode's drunken days, he'd done a lot of shameful things he'd have never considered if not under the influence. He'd made things right with God but the burning shame and guilt continued to dog his heels on the daily.

"I'll take the kitchen and work my way into the dining area." Work would help keep his mind from fixating on what might have happened with Teegan and his past. Collecting his supplies, he marched to the kitchen and began the aftermath recovery. The irony smell of blood wafted on the air, but Rhode ignored it and worked, ensuring that traces of blood didn't contaminate the other areas of the kitchen. Once he'd disinfected and deodorized the large room, he tested the area to confirm it'd been freed from pathogens.

The process wasn't difficult, but it was time-consuming and meticulous. An art he and his brothers had perfected. No one would ever know that a violent crime had been committed in the kitchen. "Clear," he called to inform his brothers that he'd finished the kitchen. As he collected his gear bag and material to work on the dining room, Teegan Albright stepped inside. Her eyes weren't as red as earlier.

She startled. "Oh!" Bringing her hand to her chest, she said, "I didn't realize anyone was in here."

"Sorry," he said, feeling a digging in his

chest again. "I, uh, just finished. It's all clear for you."

She stared at him and he shifted uncomfortably.

"Do we…do we know each other?" he asked.

Teegan shook her head. Too fast. Too hard. "I don't think so."

Lie.

Rhode had been trained to detect those as well. His suspicions had now been confirmed. He had a past with her. But from when? How long ago? Maybe she was also feeling the shame. Or she might be unsure and afraid to admit it for fear of facing embarrassment too. He'd let it pass. "If you're sure." He hung on to the last word, allowing her the chance to backtrack.

"I am. I'm sure."

"Okay," he said. What else was he supposed to do? Push and say, *Are you sure we didn't sleep together at some point in time?* Who said that other than some arrogant tool? "Again, I'm sorry about what happened to you."

"Thank you."

He pivoted to leave as the door from outside opened into the kitchen, the covered porch keeping him from getting wet. A man stalked inside, his murderous eyes focused on Teegan.

"I'll kill you!"

TWO

Teegan's heart lurched into her throat at the venomous words Glen Landoon hurled at her. Rhode Spencer jumped in front of her, his arm out like a barricade to block Teegan from harm. This was the first time since she'd returned from shopping that she actually felt safe.

"You murdered my grandmother and your own sister. It's the money, isn't it?" Glen, Lorna's grandson, said, accusation in his dark eyes. "I have news for you. You aren't getting a dime!"

"That's enough," Rhode said with a deep, menacing tone. Glen paused and sized up Rhode. Several inches taller than Glen and made like the Man of Steel. "You just threatened her, and I heard it. If you're willing to threaten homicide, then how do we know *you* didn't kill them? You clearly have murderous intent. Back. Up. Now."

Neither Glen nor his mother, Evangeline, had been fond of Teegan. Anyone new to the estate was a fortune-poacher in their eyes and they'd never shied away from being vocal about it in her presence. Truth was, it was Lorna's own family who were money-grubbers.

Teegan peered over Rhode's shoulder. "I did not kill my sister or your grandmother, Glen."

Glen glared, but didn't make another move toward her. He must have calculated that Rhode Spencer was formidable, not an opponent he would want to go up against.

"You might as well pack it up," he said. "My mother is arriving and you will not be allowed to remain in our house. I don't have to go anywhere."

Rhode's nostrils flared. "Maybe not, but it will be in your best interest to leave the kitchen immediately and to stay away from Miss Albright while she's here."

Glen eyed Rhode. If looks could kill,

Rhode would be dead on the floor and Teegan next to him. Without a word, he blew past them into the dining and foyer area.

Teegan clung to the kitchen island to keep upright. She hadn't thought about her living arrangements or the fact she was now out of a job. She was still reeling from shock. Her twin sister had been butchered and Lorna had taken a terrible fall. She'd been attacked and almost killed herself. Jobs and homes hadn't registered.

Teegan's lungs tightened and the room spun. She couldn't breathe and gasped for air.

"Teegan," Rhode murmured. "Hey." He laid a strong hand on her shoulder. "I think you may be having a panic attack. I have them sometimes. Just breathe slow. Easy."

She did as he suggested, but the thought of being homeless with two babies and no job returned and a cold sweat broke out over her body.

"Easy. Breathe."

She'd spent way too much money on gifts,

overcompensating because of her meager holidays. She'd have to return most of the presents now.

Rhode's voice was deep, smooth like velvet, and had a steadying effect on her and she did as he instructed until the episode passed and she could breathe easy again.

"Better?" he asked.

She nodded. "Thank you."

"You've had an intense and traumatizing day. It's no surprise you had a panic attack. You going to be okay now?"

She nodded again. Something about him… She'd seen him a few months ago after Sissy had been attacked, and she'd had an odd sensation then. Like she should know him, but her memories were disjointed and fuzzy.

"I'll get out of your hair now. I don't want to stay if you don't want me to."

I don't want to stay if you don't want me to.

Those words felt oddly familiar. As if he'd said them verbatim before. He turned to leave and she caught sight of the back of his head. His hair.

That head of hair. She recognized it.

Over two years ago, she'd woken to the back of that gorgeous head of hair. Everything else had been a haze as she'd slipped from the hotel room in the walk of shame, keeping quiet so as not to wake the stranger in the bed.

But she remembered the hair. Pathetic.

She also remembered one other thing.

A brass bullet that had been engraved with *Congrats. Love, Dad.*

In a scramble to leave, she'd hastily scooped up the contents from her purse, which had fallen off the dresser. Once she'd returned home, she'd found it. Teegan had accidentally swept it into her purse that morning. With no way to return it—because she hadn't even remembered his name—she'd kept it as a reminder never to touch an ounce of alcohol again. A promise she'd broken that night. That one time. After Darryl had broken their engagement three days before their courthouse marriage. She'd already been grieving her mom's death of cirrhosis and Misty had been out of control from pill popping and cycling in and out of rehab. The crushing weight and pain had tempted Teegan to break the vow with herself to never drink.

That weekend, she'd driven to Dallas to simply get away. She'd gone down to the bar to listen to live music and she'd ordered a drink. And then another, until she couldn't remember anything but fuzzy moments.

Meeting a gorgeous man.

Having a conversation with laughter, though they were only slivers of recollection. Something about twins. Names. Sadness. Flirtation. Sloppy slow dancing. Stumbling to her room. The invitation for him to come inside.

I don't want to stay, if you don't want me to.

I do. I want you to stay.

Teegan pinched the bridge of her nose as the past reared its head. A head of gorgeous hair and a face that rivaled Johnny

Depp. What on earth would she tell her children when they grew up and asked how they'd come to be? That she'd conceived them with Captain Jack Sparrow?

Rhode Spencer was her children's father, and she had no clue how to broach the subject. But she might not have to. He'd asked if they knew each other, but it was obvious he was as fuzzy as she was, or he'd been pretending to be unclear and had been feeling her out to see if she'd cop to knowing him. When she hadn't, he might have thought they were free and clear of the embarrassment. Could they play it off this way?

No.

Because she was now positive and he deserved to know he had children. If he didn't want them, fine. She would continue to raise them alone, and if he did, then they'd have a different conversation and figure out the future—but she would get to know him first. She might have made a mistake concerning herself, but now she had the children. And she wasn't going to let some guy she'd slept with once jump into their lives. What if this was a habit of his? What if he had a string of children all through Texas? She doubted it, but she wasn't taking chances with her children.

"Is there anything we can do to help you?" he asked, turning back just before the dining room.

"I don't think so." If anything, he was going to make life more complicated. She was in this alone, starting with figuring out how to handle Misty's arrangements. Her sister was dead. Gone. Not a stitch of blood kin left. She pressed the heels of her hands to her eyes. "I have a church family that can help me." Yolanda. She needed to ask if the babies could stay with her a little longer. She had a lot to figure out and unless Yolanda had turned on the news, she didn't know what had transpired today. Things had been a blur and Teegan hadn't even called.

The national news was running headlines about Lorna Landoon and social media was rampant with RIPs and how much they'd loved her movies, talking as if they'd personally known her.

Teegan had. And she'd loved her dearly. Misty hadn't made national news, other than a snippet, or been raved about online, but she was as loved by Teegan as Lorna.

"That's good that you have a church family." He scratched his head and she noticed the tattoo snaking up his forearm—a scorpion with a Scripture written along the stinger.

Another blurry memory flashed.

O death, where is thy sting.

Then she remembered a fuzzy conversation. He had said, "Scorpions are like death but I'm not afraid of dying…" Something about mistakes made…something about his faith.

She remembered that now, too, reconfirming Rhode Spencer was her baby daddy.

"Yeah." Awkward tension built between them. He shifted as if as antsy as she was to flee the kitchen and the past. He might want to escape a shameful night, but she hadn't been able to and never would.

"Teegan! Oh, Teeg!" Yolanda's alto voice echoed through the house and then she rushed into the kitchen, the beads in her long braids clicking against one another. She all but slung herself on Teegan, squeezing her like a boa constrictor. "Oh, girl. My mama called. She saw the news. I couldn't get your cell phone, so I called Harry at the stables. He told me you were here and I could come and bring the babies too. I'm so sorry."

Babies.

Yolanda had brought the babies with her.

"Where are the babies?" Teegan asked.

"Oh. Right there." She pointed to the entrance to the kitchen. Brook and River were sitting in their double stroller, their sippy cups in the cup holders and butter cookies in each hand.

But it wasn't her children that captured her attention.

It was Rhode Spencer.

He'd gone deathly quiet and was now

standing within inches of the children, his mouth agape and confusion forming a divot along his bronzed brow.

Staring at his son, he clearly saw his own reflection. Both children had his Mexican heritage in skin coloring, eyes and hair. River especially looked like Rhode from the cupid's-bow lip to the dimples.

Rhode blinked a few times then slowly met Teegan's eyes. "How...how old are they?"

She swallowed hard, her stomach churning and head buzzing. "They'll be two in January."

"Fraternal twins."

"Yes," she squeaked.

His hand trembled and he balled it into a fist. "Well, I see you have someone here to help you. I need to finish up." He walked through the kitchen, giving the children one final glance.

Passing them off.

Pretending he didn't remember or now know. But his face had revealed the hard truth. He knew he'd fathered twins. If he wanted to pass the buck and keep pretending, Teegan would let him. If he didn't want to be a dad, she wouldn't force him, but the rejection of his children throbbed deep into her bones.

"Who was that?" Yolanda's amber eyes narrowed, hands on her hips.

"No one."

He was no one. Wanted to be no one. Fine.

Her children deserved better anyway.

Twenty minutes ago, the sun had set and Rhode crumpled on the couch in the living room of his family ranch in Cedar Springs. Stone's wife, Emily, had taken Mama to her chemo treatment earlier today, and now Mama was sleeping. Emily had gone out to do some Christmas shopping. Their mother had been diagnosed with cancer last Christmas and had been battling it ever since. She was on a new round of chemo and the tumors were shrinking, which was great, but the chemo was doing her in. The oncologist said things were positive and he was confident this treatment would work, and Rhode clung to that.

He'd endured so much loss. So much pain.

His throat ached for a drink. Since he'd laid eyes on Teegan, a pool of dread had formed in his gut, the ache dogging him to dull it with a shot of bourbon. The smooth burn would numb the pain and calm his nerves. Loosen his tight muscles. He'd fought it every single minute and was fighting through it even now. Praying and repeating Scriptures that reminded him he could overcome because God was greater than the enemy of old and the bite of the bottle.

When he'd spotted the two chubby babies, it was like looking at old photographs of him and Sissy. Unmistakable. Undeniable.

And the ache turned into a raging wildfire of need.

Rhode was a father to babies he'd had no clue existed because neither he nor Teegan knew one another. If she'd wanted to inform him, she'd had no way. Shame kicked him while he was already down and a thought entered his mind: *Daddy kept a bottle of Buffalo Trace in his closet in the shoebox.*

Rhode's drinking had begun as a teenager, but after Pai died, then Daddy, it had become a crutch and coping mechanism.

A crutch made of rubber.

Instead of heading to the closet to check to see if the stash remained, he closed his eyes and prayed for strength to fight it, to be delivered from temptation, until slowly, painfully, the ache dissipated and he could open his eyes without making a beeline to the closet.

Bridge leaned on the doorframe, one ankle crossed over the other as he scrutinized him. "You fighting through it?" he asked quietly.

"Yep." Some days he was sick to death of the fight. The fact he had to fight at all.

"You want to talk about the trigger?"

Bridge was no fool. He already knew the trigger. "You saw them," Rhode murmured. "You know."

"We do. When the friend arrived, we helped her inside with the babies due to the rain and...yeah, it was pretty clear, especially after your confession about possibly having been with her."

"She doesn't remember me. I barely remember her. Timeline fits."

"You know their names?" Bridge asked.

"No." He hadn't even asked. He'd panicked, wanted a drink, and had felt absolutely wrecked by his past behavior. He'd bolted like the cowardly lion.

"Brook is the girl and River is the boy. That's kinda interesting, don't you think?"

Yeah. A fuzzy conversation surfaced. Stone. Rhode. Bridge. All places to walk or stand on. Places that get people from one point to another and are solid. Mama had done that on purpose. Appeared the conversation had stuck, if even subconsciously. His children had water names. "I have no idea what to do. I mean do I just say, 'Hey, I noticed you had babies that look like me. I think maybe we had a moment a few years ago. That was you, right?' Real romantic or mature. It's just the stupidest thing on the planet. I am a total idiot."

"I'll never not argue that you're an idiot." He smirked. "But, dude. You're a dad. You have to man up and talk to her. Maybe just say…" He grinned and shrugged at a loss. "I don't know. This is weird, but you need to have a conversation. I mean maybe they're not yours."

"We both know that's not true." He sighed. "How am I going to be a dad? Bridge, I'm broke. I have no home of my own. My private investigation biz is getting off the ground, but it's not making consistent money, and I can't go back…" Not to any police department. Not after accidentally contaminating evidence in a homicide because he'd been under the influence. The perp had walked because of Rhode and, two months later, had bludgeoned another woman. That was blood on Rhode's hands. He'd been canned, and rightly so.

That was the day he'd driven to Dallas and drunk himself stupid.

"I know," Bridge whispered. "But I don't

think being a dad is all about having hordes of money. If it was, then our dad was a failure because he never had a lot of dough. But he loved us and was a good father. I never remember what he could or couldn't buy me. I remember fishing with him, horseback riding. He taught me how to change a tire and treat a woman right. He worked hard, loved Jesus, and his family. Remember how he and Mama used to dance in the kitchen after dinner? I always groaned but, really, I loved it. I felt safe knowing they loved one another."

"'Kay, but I barely know their mother. I don't see me dancing in the kitchen with her. Pretty sure we danced at a bar though—that's real classy. This isn't that. It's not two people who fell in love, married and had a family. It's the opposite. It's two people who were too dumb to restrain themselves." He hung his head. "I always wanted a family. I'm not going to run from it—forever."

"Good. Because I think a couple of babies would make Mama feel better again.

And they are pretty stinkin' cute, bro. You did good. Well, you know what I mean."

"Yeah." He laughed, but it wasn't funny. "Can't blame the babies for our mistake or hold it against them. And it's pretty clear I'd produce adorable children."

Bridge snorted at Rhode's teasing. "Helps that their mom is a knockout."

It was an innocent statement but Rhode's blood heated a degree. "Yeah, well don't go making moves. My kids don't need an Uncle Daddy." They needed their father. Rhode. He stood. "You think it's too late to go over there?"

"You know, Rhode, I don't think it's ever too late to make something wrong right." He slapped his thighs. "I'm eating some leftovers for dinner and going to bed." On the way out, he paused. "What are you getting Sissy for Christmas? I feel like we need to outdo Beau, but how do you outdo a man with millions?"

Rhode laughed. "I have no stinking clue."

"Well, I can always count on you for great

ideas." Bridge rolled his eyes then sobered. "If you feel like you want to drink, please call me. Praying for you."

Tears burned the backs of Rhode's eyes. "Thanks. I will."

As he geared up to return to the Landoon estate and face the music, his throat started the dry ache again. God would get him through this. God was in this. He had to be, or Rhode was doomed.

Grabbing his keys, he headed to the vehicle and drove to the estate, his stomach in a million little pretzels, all twisted and corkscrewed.

He parked where he had earlier. The rain was now a steady sheet but the thunderstorms had subsided. Teegan's car was in the drive. Guess the Glen guy hadn't forced her out yet. That man grated Rhode's nerves. How dare he threaten Teegan? Or accuse her of murdering for money. Seemed he was the one who wanted his hand in the coffers.

He did not like that guy. At all.

As he approached the front door, he heard a bloodcurdling scream.

Teegan's scream.

THREE

Someone had appeared in the second floor sitting room.

Out of nowhere!

This time he wore a ski mask in place of his plastic jester mask, but the knife in his hand appeared the same. Big and shiny and sharp.

She raced toward the grand staircase, away from the nursery where the babies slept. They were early to rise and early to bed. He chased after her and she was going to lead him outside, away from the children. But she stumbled on the stairs, letting out a shriek. She tumbled down several before she crashed against the wooden rail.

Images of Lorna's fall popped into her mind and she scrambled to her feet, the attacker coming right for her. She dashed through the foyer and was reaching for the doorknob when the door flung open, knocking her off balance.

Rhode Spencer was there.

His sight landed on the stairs where the intruder stood as startled as Teegan had been to see Rhode. Rhode's eyes glazed over in a hot fury that burned through Teegan's bones. He bolted past Teegan, lightly brushing her shoulder in comfort, and rushed toward the man with the knife, who was already sprinting up the stairs.

No way he'd escape now.

Unless he made it to the back staircase and down them before Rhode reached him.

Her babies were upstairs and helpless. Except they weren't.

Their father was upstairs.

But she was their mother. And their father didn't want to be one. He all but flew out of here earlier upon seeing them. Without weighing the consequences, nothing but the twins on her mind, she took the stairs two at a time. Halfway up, Rhode appeared.

He held a gun in his right hand. "I think

he made it down the back staircase. I followed and went outside. Didn't see him. But I want to clear the place before I call it safe."

"My babies. I need to be with my babies." Her heart raced and no one, including Rhode, was going to keep her from them.

"Okay. Go to them and stay in the room until I let you know it's safe."

Teegan followed him upstairs and he escorted her to the nursery. River and Brook were sound asleep in their crib, and he silently checked the nooks, crannies and closet. Then he nodded and slipped out of the room, leaving her to keep watch over the babies. Had the intruder known children were present? Would a monster with a knife even care?

After what seemed like an eternity, Rhode returned. "All clear," he whispered, glancing at the crib and his sleeping babes. "Doors are locked. I've called Dom and he's on his way with the Cedar Springs forensic team. They'll want to comb for evidence, and Dom will need a statement. It's safe though."

For now. Someone wanted her dead and maybe even her children. The word *safe* did little to comfort her. Not when all she kept seeing was a big sharp knife coming for her.

Teegan motioned to the door and they left the room. Outside the babies' room was a hall that led to an open loft area with a couch, love seat and rocking recliner. The back wall behind the couch was lined with floor-to-ceiling bookshelves. Lorna had been an avid reader—a romantic at heart— and hundreds of Harlequin romances lined the shelves along with Agatha Christie mysteries and some classics.

"What are you doing here?" Teegan asked, covering her heart with her hand, hoping the racing would slow. "I'm glad. Don't get me wrong."

His sad eyes and apologetic smile sent her heart into a tremor.

"I, uh, came by because we need to talk, and I'm fairly sure you know why."

He searched her eyes and she reluctantly nodded.

"Hold on." She left the loft and hurried to her bedroom on the opposite side of the nursery. She retrieved the bullet that belonged to Rhode and grabbed the baby monitor as well. When she returned, she held the bullet out to him. "I think this belongs to you," she murmured.

He rolled it between his fingers. "My dad gave me this when I finished the police academy. I thought I'd lost it. But... I couldn't remember where. Now, I know." He closed his fist over it and peered into her eyes. "I don't know what to say."

Teegan was speechless, too, and her nerves worked overtime. Between this awkward conversation and the fact someone had tried to kill her and might still want to, she was overwhelmed and a ball of knots. "I don't remember that night much, to be honest. I'd been dumped three days before my wedding—I probably told you that but—"

"We don't remember," he whispered.

"No. I was stupid. Angry. Hurt. Depressed. And that was the first time I'd ever drank in my life. My mom was a drunk until she died. But in that moment, I didn't care, and I got drunk fast. Everything else is hazy."

"I understand."

What if he thought this was normal behavior for her? Would he want to take the children away? He didn't understand, but needed to. "I broke a promise to myself that night. But since then, I haven't touched a single drop of alcohol."

Rhode nodded. "I believe you, and I'm sorry. For then and for earlier today." He glanced away. "I thought you might be familiar when I saw you a few months ago, but I wasn't sure then or until I saw the babies. That's when I knew and I… I panicked."

She appreciated his honesty and owning up to running away. But he had returned, and it had been perfect timing. She could not let this jester hurt her children—or her.

"It's a lot to process, and I've had plenty of time, so I get it."

"I appreciate the grace, Teegan. I don't deserve it."

"I guess that's why it's called grace." She half smiled. "I thought I'd put that night behind me until eight weeks later. With no way of contacting you, I wasn't sure what to do. I couldn't even remember your name." Shame flushed her cheeks.

"I'm not mad you didn't contact me. That you didn't—couldn't—find me."

That was a relief. "I don't want anything from you. So, you don't have to worry about that. I'm not going to force back child support or anything."

"No," he said and shook his head. "I want to make sure you have what you need—what they need. I'm not a heartless man. Just a… I don't what I am. Sorry. That's what I am. I'm so sorry. Two babies. That can't be easy for you."

It wasn't. "We're making do. Lorna was good to us, but, now I'm not sure where we'll go. Glen's mother, Evangeline, did come by and she gave me a whole forty-eight hours to evacuate. Because she knows I have babies. Whatever." Tears filled her eyes and she wanted to kick herself for not being stronger. "Yolanda, my friend who brought the babies back, said I could stay—"

"Stay with me." He reached out from the couch where he perched and grabbed her hand. "Please."

Teegan froze. "I…uh, I don't do things like that. That was a drunken one-time mistake."

Rhode stood. "No. No. I don't mean that. I mean my family ranch. My brother Stone and his wife live there, and my mom. She'd love to meet the babies. My other brother, Bridge, told me they're named Brook and River."

She grinned. "Yeah. I liked the idea of them having meaning together. Both bodies of water. Fresh springs representing new life. Living water. I kinda feel we talked about that?"

"I think so." He kicked at the floor runner. "I'd like to meet them, Teegan. Have a chance to know them. I'm not a bad man. I just made some bad choices."

Teegan never thought she'd find their father. Sharing the kids now seemed odd. And yet a sliver of her found relief in knowing she might not be alone. But she didn't truly know Rhode Spencer. Spending time with him and his family might be what she needed to get to know him. She might have made a one-night mistake, but what about him? Was it a one-time drink that had blurred his moral lines? Was drinking a part of his life? She would not allow the babies to be around someone who couldn't control his drink. Like Mom. How was she supposed to ask about that? She decided to be bold. It was her children involved here.

"The drinking. That night was a one-time thing for me, but what about you?" Rhode appeared to be honorable. He'd already protected her twice and he'd returned to own up to his responsibility.

"I haven't had a drop of alcohol since

that night either. Teetotaler," he said and glanced away.

Tightness lightened in her shoulders. Good. That was good to know. "I guess we need to get to know each other better." Her face heated. How much more could they know one another? This was beyond uncomfortable and weird, and it was no one's fault but their own.

Rhode returned to the couch and she sat opposite him on the love seat, placing the baby monitor on the end table. "So...you work with your brothers in the aftermath recovery business?"

"I do, and I'm a private detective."

"How'd you decide that?" she asked and rubbed her hands on her thighs.

"I used to be a homicide detective with Cedar Springs but—"

"But you went into the family business. That's nice. I always wanted a tight-knit family—a big family—but it was just me and Misty. Man, I miss her so much. I haven't even had time to grieve."

Rhode cleared his throat. "I lost my oldest sister, Paisley, about five years ago now. She was murdered by a serial killer, and it was made to look like a suicide. We thought for four years she'd taken her own life until Stone's now wife, a Texas Ranger in the Public Integrity Unit, worked a case that connected Paisley to a serial killer. They caught him. We also lost our father."

"I'm so sorry." She sat quietly a few moments before speaking again. "I remember reading about that. Does it ever get easier—the loss?"

Rhode shook his head. "No. Just different. You eventually sort of adapt."

The doorbell rang.

Rhode stood. "That'll be Dom and the forensic team." They headed downstairs, Teegan with the monitor in hand. She opened the front door and Dom DeMarco stood with a kind smile on his face.

With all the police and Rhode here, she should feel calmer and safer, but she didn't. Leaving this estate might be the best thing but that didn't mean the jester wouldn't or couldn't find her. Why? Why her? Why Misty?

"We meet again, Miss Albright." Dom took her statement, and she told the CSI team where she'd been and that her babies were asleep in the second room on the right upstairs. They went to work and Dom left Teegan with Rhode to join the forensic team.

"You want a cup of tea or coffee?" Teegan asked. "I could use a cup of tea." Her nerves buzzed and her heart was stuck in her throat. "I have decaf, since it's evening."

"Sure. Tea sounds fine."

Rhode followed her into the kitchen where she went to work filling a kettle with water. "You ever ride Miss Landoon's horses?"

"No. I'm skittish. I fell off a horse once during a petting zoo at the school and broke my arm. I haven't ridden since but I do like to go out to the stables and see them, watch them graze. What about you?"

"I like horses, and dogs. I ride often. The horses—not the dogs." A sense of humor.

She liked that; a few memories surfaced of her laughing at the bar, though his face was still fuzzy.

"This is weird." She might as well be honest.

"It really is." His laugh was nervous. "But I'm glad to know that I have kids, Teegan. I don't shirk responsibility and I appreciate your wariness about me concerning them. That's being a good mom. Protecting the kids."

Teegan almost cried again. Other than from Lorna, she hadn't heard she was doing a good job at being a mom; she didn't have a role model. She only knew she didn't want to be anything like her own parents. Often, she felt inadequate and lost. Alone. "Thank you. I'm trying. I'm a Christ follower, and raising them in church, though you wouldn't have known it from that time in Dallas. I was in a really dark place and sometimes when…"

"You're in a dark place, you do dark things you never thought you would," he finished for her.

"Yes. Exactly that." What a relief to know he didn't count her sin against her like so many others had.

"I'm a Christ follower too. And I get dark places. Dark things. I thank God for grace and forgiveness or we'd all be in eternal trouble."

She smiled then. Good. He was a man of faith. A fallible man. But one of faith. She could work with that. It would be good for the babies. "Amen to that."

They sat quietly at the table until he finally spoke again, changing the subject.

"Teegan, who is after you?" He leaned forward with his elbows on his knees. "The theory was that your sister borrowed trouble and it found her. But this attack with yet another knife…is it possible—and I even hate to suggest it—is it possible that your sister's killer had a case of mistaken identity? That you were his target, not her? You are identical twins."

She hadn't thought of that, but with the fact she'd been nearly killed again… "I don't know." Fear crept into her veins and

turned her blood cold. "I can't think of anyone who might want me dead." Or Lorna.
Although her fall appeared to have been an
accident. But because Misty was murdered,
they hadn't ruled it out yet. Plus, they still
had to do an autopsy. She shuddered.

"Tell me about that jester mask. He wasn't
wearing it tonight, but he was earlier."

"It was one of those plastic ones, no hat
or bells. It was white with black diamonds
around the eyes and a ruby-red mouth that
stretched into an evil grin. It was horrifying!"

Rhode took one of her hands in his. "I'm
sorry you went through that. Does that
mean anything to you? A jester mask?"

She shook her head.

"What about the Texas bluebonnets that
were in the blood? Did you see them?"

If she did, she didn't remember. She
shook her head again. "I know he must have
brought them. Lorna said the state flower
is overrated and refused to grow them or
have them in the house. She was funny that
way. A real card, you know?" She already

missed her terribly. And Misty. It was almost impossible to imagine life without her other half, even if they had been estranged for years.

"I used to sneak onto the property as a kid—with my brothers—and search for the rumored treasure." His voice was wistful. Seemed like everyone wanted a piece of that pie, believing a pile of money would solve their problems and provide security. Even Teegan had wished for a cash cow, but she'd learned from her scraping by that God alone was her safe place and security. She might not have had much, but she'd never starved or gone naked. She reminded herself of that now. God would take care of her like He always had.

"I sneaked onto the property once too," she confessed. "We grew up in Round Rock, so it was about a forty-minute drive here."

"Never found the treasure then?" Rhode smiled and she realized he was serious.

"No. I wish."

"Same. You come out here with a boy?"

She blushed at his teasing. "Hardly. I wasn't as popular as my sister."

"Never even asked to a dance?"

"Once or twice but I never went."

"Two left feet?" he teased.

Teegan snickered. "No. I just… I didn't like leaving my mom alone. If she spent too much time alone, she'd find a bottle. Go out and buy one. Misty didn't seem to care, but I did. I wanted her to stay sober. I needed her to."

Rhode dropped his head and his eyes filled with sorrow. "I'm sorry. Alcoholism is a wicked monster unleashed, breathing its fire and devouring anyone in its path."

"You've known a drunk then?"

"A drunk," he whispered. "Yeah. Yeah, I have."

"Then you know why I've never touched a drop and would never let our children be in that kind of environment."

Rhode let out a long, heavy breath. "I do." He sat up and the pain etched over his face turned resolute. "I want to take this case.

Pro bono. You're in danger, which means the children are too."

"Really?" Was he serious?

"Yeah. Cedar Springs is down a detective and they could use the help. I can work with Dom off the books."

"You don't want to go back? I mean if they're short." Maybe he made more money going solo.

He looked away and she caught a flicker again in his eyes. She knew the look. One of loss and regret. "It's a complicated story for another time, but our agency is doing well, and it's personal to me."

"Alright then."

"I'm putting that Glen Landoon on the top of the list. Anyone else belong there?"

Teegan wasn't a fan of Lorna's grandson, but she wasn't sure he was the jester. "He's a lot of bark with no bite. His mother, Evangeline, is all bite with no bark. Truth is, the whole family has been estranged from Lorna. They visit because they want her money, and she knew that. She wasn't stupid. In fact, she was quite brilliant. Did you know she was allowed to help direct a movie? Unheard of in that time! She created literacy foundations as well as programs for theater for girls. She was ahead of her time, that's for sure." Teegan admired Lorna and even more so once Lorna became a Christian. "She traveled the world helping children learn to read and use their creative abilities. She even wrote a play they could perform that shared the gospel with other children."

"She really was amazing. And the money trail is always the first one to go down." He looked around again. "This place is massive and you shouldn't be here alone. I can bunk in the sitting room. Keep y'all safe for the night. Then consider staying on the family ranch with us. My mama's heart would be so happy to be around the grandbabies. She's been sick. Cancer. I think it would cheer her up."

How could Teegan say no to that?

She couldn't.

"Okay, then."

She wasn't sure what was scarier. Meeting Rhode's family or facing a killer.

Rhode awoke to baby chatter and Teegan's soft hushes. Last night, he'd slept on the couch downstairs, as promised, and had done perimeter sweeps every thirty minutes. He'd only dozed about an hour ago.

He rubbed his dry, gritty eyes and stretched his stiff neck then rose and combed his fingers through his hair before popping two breath mints.

Barely 6:00 a.m.

The smell of toast rumbled his stomach as he entered the kitchen. The babies sat in identical high chairs, each with a plate of scrambled eggs and triangle slices of toast with butter. Brook gummed her toast, a glob of butter on her chubby pink cheek, and River banged his little plate on the tray, his eggs smooshed everywhere.

"Did we wake you?" Teegan asked. She'd dressed in an oversize sweatshirt of the Grinch decorating a Christmas tree and black leggings. Her hair was in its usual bun on her head, with a few strands hanging.

"No. I wasn't sleeping sound. Just dozing." He glanced at the children. Brook had fisted her toast and was staring at him with big, brown eyes while River continued to beat the eggs into oblivion.

"Yes," he said to Brook softly and inched closer, "I'm someone new."

She raised her toast and said, "Sose."

Rhode's insides became as mushy as River's eggs. This was the most beautiful little girl ever born on the planet. "You got sose. Yu-ummm," he said, dragging out the word. Rhode didn't have a ton of experience with babies, but he'd had baby cousins growing up and he'd always gotten a kick out of them.

"Umm," Brook mimicked, her smile revealing four perfectly adorable teeth.

River joined in. "Ma-ma. Ma-ma."

Teegan turned from the sink where she was washing the pan. "What you want, baby?"

"Ma-ma. Ma-ma."

She grinned. "Yes, Mama's cooking."

He knocked his sippy cup of apple juice from the tray and Rhode returned it. "Here ya go, bud." He rustled his thick cap of dark hair. "You're gonna break every heart in Texas, dude," he muttered.

"I hope not," Teegan said. "I hope to teach him how to be a better man than one who simply breaks hearts."

Rhode agreed and turned. "I just meant he's a good-looking guy and—"

Her smile was soft and full, creating a ripple effect through his system. "I know what you meant. It's okay. You hungry? Want coffee? I have until eight to be out of here. I packed us up last night. Not like I have much."

"I'll grab a cup of coffee, but you don't need to cook for me, Teegan. Thanks though." He headed for the counter and poured a mug of black coffee. "Have you decided on arrangements for your sister?" He hated bringing it up, but she was alone and might need some help. "If you need anything, I can be there for you."

"Thank you. That means a lot." She dropped her head as a choked sob forced its way from her lips. "We have no family. Misty cycled through friends and, once she used them up, they abandoned her. I don't have a lot of money, so I called the funeral home director back last night as well. I'm having her cremated and her ashes will stay with me. No service or anything. There's no one to attend but me." She wiped a few tears. "Lorna put her wishes for rest in a will." Her lips quivered and the dam broke loose.

Rhode gently wrapped his arm around her, unsure if she'd be cool with his comfort. She surprised him by turning into his chest and allowing him to draw her closer.

"Let it out. We ain't goin' nowhere." At least not until eight.

Teegan's world had crumbled in a day. One horrific and painful thing after the next. No Lorna. No Misty. No home. No job.

Rhode tightened his hold on Teegan as the babies banged sippy cups, tossed eggs on the floor and squealed in utter delight at their mess. River rubbed eggs in his hair and Brook threw her wet, soggy crust onto the floor. No wonder his mom had always been exhausted when they were little. This was only breakfast and the sun hadn't risen yet.

Finally, Teegan's sobs quieted and she peered up through blue watery eyes, shifting his heart like it was a fault line. Rhode scraped a strand of hair glued by tears from her cheek then tucked it behind her ear. "You're not alone, Teegan. I'm not going anywhere."

"Thank you," she whispered, breaking from his arms and leaving a chilly empty space that unsettled him. "I have to clean up and bathe the babies."

"I can help. If they'll let me."

"They will. Neither are bashful. Brook is more vocal and picking up words faster than River, but he makes up for it in grunts and throwing things."

Rhode chuckled. He'd been a rowdy boy too. Teegan snagged a clean washcloth and,

as she ran it under warm water, Rhode unrolled several paper towels from the holder.
They worked in tandem washing up the
children and the high chairs. While Teegan
picked eggs from River's jet-black hair,
Rhode lifted Brook from her highchair, toast
crumbs sticking to her pink footie pajamas.

"Hey, darlin', you want to get a bath?"

"Ba-ba-ba."

"You're smart. Like your mama." He
grinned when Teegan glanced his way.

"How do you know I'm smart?"

"Because these babies are smart, and they
sure didn't get it from me." He ran his finger down his daughter's cheek. How did
one man lose his heart to a baby this fast?
There was nothing he wouldn't do for these
two. He was like a volcano of love and pro-
tectiveness waiting to erupt.

"I don't know about that. Detectives and
private detectives have to be smart to catch
killers." She settled River on her hip and
they carried the babies to the stairs.

Teegan sighed. "The elevator is broken,
but I don't mind too much. Stairs benefit

me healthwise, and now I have no choice. Can't be lazy on purpose."

Rhode smirked and they started up the stairs. Teegan was absolutely perfect to him, but he refrained from scoping her out. Not exactly respectful, and he didn't want to flash on any memories he shouldn't.

Once upstairs in Teegan's east wing, they bathed and dressed the kids then packed up the rest of their things, including the breakdown of the crib. Last night, Stone had swapped out Rhode's SUV for his pickup so they would have more room for Teegan and the babies' belongings.

By eight on the dot, Evangeline Landoon, her son, Glen, and her grandson, Charlie—who looked like a live Ken doll—stood in the foyer. Evangeline was tall, with wide blue eyes and long lashes. Her platinum-blond bob was a little longer in the front and her grubby hand was held out for Teegan to deposit the keys. She raised her sharp chin, peering down at Teegan. "You can pick up your check on Friday."

That was it. No sentiments about car-ing for Lorna these past six months. Not a single word. But it wasn't Evangeline's arrogance that caught Rhode's eye. It was Charlie's lecherous sneer that raised his hackles.

Teegan carefully handed over her keys and silently walked to her car. They buckled up the babies. And Rhode turned back one last time to see them with their smug smiles evicting them from the property. "Let's get out of here. Just follow me."

Rhode left the estate and, as he neared the family ranch, his stomach twisted and turned. Anticipation. Nerves. Everyone would be at the ranch. Bridge lived in a cabin on the backside of the property, but he always came up to the house in the mornings for coffee and a muffin. Stone and his wife, Emily, lived in the ranch house, with Mama. Sissy lived about a half a mile away. Beau had built them a new home before their wedding.

He pulled into the driveway and Teegan parked behind him, but she remained inside the car. He approached and she rolled down the window. "I'm nervous," she said. "I don't want your family to think I'm some kind of tramp."

He opened her car door and clasped her hands, gently coaxing her out of the driver's seat. "You are no such thing, and no one is going to judge you." Not when they could have judged Rhode so much harder and never had. "We were broken people who did a broken thing. It doesn't define us. And we got something good out of it in the end."

She nodded. "You're a good man, I think."

Oh, for grace… And she wouldn't think that if she knew he, too, battled addiction like her mom. But that was a conversation for another time. Once she'd gotten to know him—the real him. "Let's go see the fam. Also, prepare to eat again. My mom usually feels pretty good the day after chemo. It's about day three or four when the fatigue and nausea hit. She's probably baked something. Or Emily has, in which case, just smile and pretend to like it."

She laughed as they hauled the babies out of the car seats and went inside.

As predicted, the whole family was home and at the large farm table in the kitchen, no doubt awaiting their arrival. "Everyone," Rhode said, "this is Teegan Albright, and these most adorable things you have ever laid eyes on are Brook and River. My kids."

Mama approached first and hugged Teegan. "I'm Marisol, and you must call me that. Welcome to the family, Teegan. We're happy to have you and the babes. I love their names. So perfectly perfect, dear."

Teegan visibly relaxed and thanked her. "Would you like to hold him?"

"I would."

Teegan handed River over to Marisol and he went right to her, grabbing at her bottom lip with a slobbery grin.

The whole family oohed and aahed over the babies, passing them around like hors d'oeuvres and baby-talking them. Even his gruffest brother, Stone, fell into the baby trap. "Are you so cute? Yes, you are so cute."

Rhode would rib him over it later.

Mama had made cinnamon rolls from scratch and the house smelled like yeast and cinnamon…and the holidays.

Sissy and Emily drilled Teegan with baby questions, and Stone gave Emily a look that said he was ready for fatherhood. Beau kissed Sissy's head when she held Brook and they exchanged a glance. Well. Well. Well. Rhode thought he'd noticed a rosy glow in his sister's cheeks these past few weeks. No secrets between them, not with twin radar. But he'd let them announce it on their own.

Were there secrets between Teegan and Misty?

Someone wanted one of them dead. He had to find out if Misty had been the intended target or if it had been a case of mistaken identity. Once he concluded that, he could dig deeper.

Teegan's phone rang. She frowned and answered. "Yes, of course. When? And why me?" She listened and nodded. "So, I have to be?" She tucked the corner of her bottom lip into her mouth. "Okay then," she said weakly and ended the call.

"Is everything alright?" Rhode asked.

"I don't know. That was one of Lorna's attorneys, Scott Carmichael. I have to be at the Landoon estate at ten this morning for a reading of the will." She rubbed her hands on her thighs. "I don't understand."

"She left you something," Bridge said through a mouthful of cinnamon roll.

"But why? What could she possibly want to give me?"

"She loved you," Sissy said. "You know that. She talked about you all the time to me. She considered you a granddaughter. I think it's great."

"Well, the family won't. Evangeline, Glen and Charlie detest me. Dexter—Evangeline's brother—and his grandson, Peter, don't, but I'm not sure how they'll react."

"What about Peter's parents?" Rhode asked.

"No one knew who Peter's father was. Dexter's daughter—Peter's mom—died in a horse accident when he was young. Dexter raised Peter."

"So much tragedy," Marisol said.

Teegan nodded. "Dexter and Evangeline are fraternal twins."

"My, that's a lot of twins," Marisol commented.

Teegan smirked. "It's one of the reasons Lorna offered me the job. The twins reminded her of Evangeline and Dexter."

"Do you know anything about them?" Rhode asked.

"Peter and Charlie are more like brothers than cousins, and he has a hand in the thoroughbred business as well. Peter's actually quite nice. A little quiet. He visits Lorna more than the others. But I don't know how he'll respond if she leaves me something he might want."

"Maybe it's the treasure," Bridge said, his eyes alight with excitement.

"Get over that," Rhode said. "You'd think you were still fourteen."

Bridge shrugged and snagged another cinnamon roll.

Teegan clutched her stomach. "I'm going to be in bloody water with sharks. I dread it."

"I'll go with you." Rhode laid a hand on her shoulder.

"I can keep the babies," Sissy offered, and Emily and Mama nodded enthusiastically.

"Are you sure? I don't want to be a burden," Teegan said.

"Oh, child. This is family, not a burden." Marisol bounced River on her lap and played patty-cake with him. "We'll be right as rain. And the children will be good and spoiled."

Teegan's eyes filled with moisture. "You have no idea how much that means to me." She looked at Rhode. "We better get going then. I'll follow you in case you need to go, but I want to leave the car seats."

Rhode checked his watch. It was after nine. He grabbed his keys, then removed the car seats from Teegan's car and left them for Sissy in case they needed to take the babies somewhere. On their way to the vehicles, a foreboding swept over Rhode.

What if Lorna and Misty had been murdered over Lorna's fortune?

But the jester got the wrong sister.

FOUR

Teegan's stomach lurched as she pulled into the circular drive at Lorna's estate. Rhode parked his modest SUV beside luxury sedans and sports cars that cost more than the average American's yearly income. She met him at the front door, and he laid his hands on her shoulders. "These people are nothing but skin and bones like us. But I can tell you, from running in these elite circles, that they love the smell of inferiority. If you don't go in there with your head up, like you belong, they'll attempt to eat you alive. I won't let it come to that."

Teegan peered into his rich dark eyes, the resoluteness infusing her with the strength she desperately needed. "I'll try. I'm so far removed from this kind of wealth and life that it's intimidating."

"I understand. Trust me. Head up." He lightly lifted her chin and searched her eyes, holding her head until he seemed to realize she was ready.

"Head up," she whispered, and he removed his hold on her chin and nodded once.

Rhode didn't bother to knock. He opened the door and swaggered inside as if he belonged there more than anyone else. She admired the boldness, and it helped her straighten her shoulders and walk with more authority than she felt.

An attractive man with broad shoulders and dressed in a fitted and flashy suit met them in the foyer, his chestnut hair cut short but trendy. A few fine lines crinkled around his amber eyes as he grinned.

He waited a moment, but when Teegan didn't speak, he held out his hand. "Teegan, I presume. Scott Carmichael of Lindenstein, Carter and Brumm. I'll be handling the reading of the will today."

"Nice to meet you."

The lawyer eyed Rhode, waiting for an

introduction. Teegan wasn't sure how to answer this one. "Um…"

"I'm Rhode Spencer. Teegan's fiancé."

Her what? Teegan opened her mouth but remained silent.

"I see," Scott Carmichael said. He dropped his gaze to Teegan's left hand, but Rhode had already discreetly taken it in his, hiding the fact she wore no engagement ring. "Follow me. Everyone's in Lorna's sitting room awaiting your arrival."

Rhode squeezed her hand and whispered, "Sorry, had to improvise. Mentioning that I'm a PI would be frowned on, and saying I'm your baby daddy didn't really feel right either."

She grinned, unable to help herself. "I don't think I would have put it quite like that." Although it was exactly like that.

His lopsided smirk swirled into her belly. Rhode Spencer. Mercy, he was beautiful. Men didn't care for that description. They preferred rugged or hot. But Rhode was exceptionally beautiful, and she was swiftly learning he was every bit as beautiful on the inside too.

Surely, she wasn't crushing on her children's father. Right now, the last thing she needed was a romantic entanglement. She was homeless and the list went on. Still... she couldn't help the way he made her feel. Not that he felt the same. He'd never once mentioned anything personal. Only interaction due to keeping her and the twins safe.

Inside the sitting room, Glen and Evangeline stood by the piano and paused their conversation when they spotted her. They might as well be wolves licking their chops as the chicken ventured away from the henhouse. Rumor around the stables was Evangeline never married because she didn't want to share her piece of the Landoon pie if a marriage didn't work. Of course, Teegan had no idea about Evangeline's personal life.

Glen's son rolled his eyes at seeing her and sipped his whiskey neat.

Dexter was in Lorna's favorite chair, scrolling on his phone as if bored with the event. Peter gave her a weak wave and smile, but at least ventured over to talk. Poor Peter had lost so much of his family and never known his father. His grandmother—Dexter's wife—passed a year ago to cancer and now Lorna.

"Teegan, how are you?"

"I've been better."

He touched her shoulder. "I was in Dallas when everything happened. I'm so sorry for your loss—of my great-grandmother and your sister." His sharp brown eyes met Rhode's, and he extended his hand. "Peter Landoon. I'm Lorna's great-grandson."

"I gathered that." Rhode accepted the handshake. "I'm Rhode Spencer, Teegan's fiancé."

"Oh." Peter's dark eyebrows raised and his mouth parted. "I didn't realize."

"It's new," Rhode said. "But we've known each other awhile. I'm the twins' daddy."

Peter's mouth hardened. "I see. Well, welcome." He excused himself and returned to his father, who continued scrolling on his phone.

"He have a thing for you?" Rhode asked. "How old is he?"

"Late thirties, like Charlie. Actually, he may be early forties. And no, he doesn't." He'd once invited her to ride horses, but Lorna had interrupted with the fact she was being paid to work. Peter had politely seen himself out. He'd never asked again.

A throat cleared and Teegan spun around. Harry Doyle stood with his cowboy hat in hand, dirty work jeans, and weathered skin. "I, uh, I was called to be here?" he said, but it felt more like a question. He was as out of place in this hoity-toity environment as Teegan. Standing beside him was her friend and estate manager, Olivia Wheaton. She said nothing, but waved at Teegan.

"Yes, please, everyone come and have a seat."

"Why are they here?" Evangeline asked. "Let them get their treats and go."

The lawyer cleared his throat and caught Teegan's eye, silently apologizing. "Miss Landoon, I'll get to that."

Evangeline huffed and Dexter shot her a warning look, his phone still in hand.

Scott began reading. "'I, Lorna Landoon, a resident of Cedar Springs, Texas, declare this to be my Last Will and Testament, and revoke all previous wills and codicils, made by me, either jointly or severally. I am of sound mind and not under any duress, and this expresses my wishes.'"

"What does that mean? 'Revoke all previous wills'?" Glen asked.

"It means that anything previously written before this is void," Scott said.

Evangeline's face paled and she touched the hollow of her throat. "And when was this new will written?"

"November twenty-ninth of this year, ma'am."

The family exchanged worried glances. Had Lorna amended her will? Sylvia Bondurant, the senior attorney on her team, had visited a few times these past two months, but Teegan hadn't realized it might be to amend or change the will.

Scott read the amounts of money Lorna

had willed to charities and organizations. "Before I announce the executor of her estate and the divvying up of money, property and assets, she'd like me to read this letter, which was written on November twenty-ninth of this year."

Scott opened the letter.

"'My dear family,
You undoubtedly thought I'd never kick the bucket but clearly I have.'"

Teegan imagined Lorna's upper-crust mid-Atlantic accent speaking the words.

"'I've made a lot of mistakes in my life,'" Scott read with perfect enunciation. "'One was staying in Hollywood too long. Fulfilling your desires without hesitation. By the time I realized what was truly important in life, you'd already become part of a dark world full of selfish ambition, greed, and, well, quite frankly, bratty behavior. I regret that.

I own it as I own all my sins. I never

should have given you each a trust of ten million when you hit twenty-one. You never learned hard work. Not like I did before I hit it big. You don't know what integrity or nobility means. You do not know any life other than one of privilege—which isn't a bad thing, children, if it's balanced. And that is why, through diligent prayer and consideration, I am leaving you one-hundred and fifty thousand dollars. And that is all. Whatever is left of your trust is yours.'"

Gasps echoed and Glen shot to his feet, his cheeks redder than a male cardinal. Scott continued.

"'I make Teegan Elizabeth Albright the executor, and I leave to her all my property, estate, which includes every asset on the estate, including the thoroughbred business, as well as all my accounts domestic and foreign. Harry Doyle has done well by the horses and me, and he is a good man. Therefore, I request that he stay on as the manager of the stables and I give him forty percent shares in the business. Well done, thy good and faithful servant. To Olivia, I give you the option to remain on as estate manager and two million dollars regardless. You've been a gem to me. Well done, thy good and faithful servant.'"

Scott finished reading, but Teegan's mind buzzed as she tried to process.

Lorna had left everything—every single thing except forty percent of the thoroughbreds—to her. Why? Why would she do this?

"This is an outrage!" Evangeline shrieked. "My mother would never do this to her family."

Glen insulted Teegan with names. "What did you do to my grandmother? How did you swindle what is rightfully ours? I demand to revoke this will. My grandmother was clearly not sound in mind even though she said otherwise."

"I have to agree," Charlie said.

Dexter sighed. "We will contest this, Mr. Carmichael. You'll hear from my lawyer this afternoon. Peter."

Peter stood but said nothing as they left.

"Well, I'm not leaving this house." Evangeline crossed her arms over her chest, her chin raised. Glen and Charlie flanked her in a united front.

"I'm afraid that is up to Miss Albright. She's the owner of the property and the home," Scott said.

"You will pay for this," Charlie Landoon snarled and stalked toward her.

Rhode stood again as her barrier. "Don't you threaten her. Or you'll have me to deal with, and that's not a threat. It's a promise."

Charlie held his gaze, a murderous glint in his eye.

"And you'll need to drop your keys on the table on your way out. All of you. Give back Teegan's keys as well."

Charlie backed down and stormed from

the house, his father glaring at Teegan as he followed, the sound of keys crashing to the floor echoed. Only Evangeline, Olivia and Harry Doyle remained.

"You'll regret this, Miss Albright," Evangeline said. "You may have the house for the moment, but when I'm finished, you and those little babies of yours will be on the street, and from there I don't care what happens to you, but you will not win." She cast her gaze on Rhode. "That's not a threat," she stressed. "It's a promise." She threw the keys down at their feet and raged away.

"I don't understand," Teegan said. "Why me?" She slumped in the chair by the window.

"I don't know, Miss Albright. She also left you a private letter." The lawyer handed it to her.

"What are the chances they contest and win?" Rhode asked.

Scott inhaled and tapped the papers. "The lawyer who drew up the documents would have to testify that Lorna was of sound mind. They will interview doctors as they investigate her mental health. If she was as sharp as it appears in her letter, I'd say nil. This is all yours, Miss Albright. I left the papers with the financial numbers on the piano up there. You're a very wealthy woman now." He nodded once and exited the room.

Harry and Olivia approached. Olivia leaned down. "Lorna knew what she was doing. I'm not surprised she didn't give them a dime. I am surprised she left me what she did. I'll stay on if you'd like. I enjoy the job."

Teegan grasped her hand. "I would love that. Thank you. Just keep doing what you've always done. Harry, same for you, I guess."

He stood shaking his head. "I'll be where I always am if you need me."

They both left, leaving Teegan and Rhode alone.

"How wealthy am I?"

Rhode picked up the papers from the piano and flipped through them, then low whistled. "Let's just say the twins can go to an Ivy League school hundreds of times if they want and then some."

Tears filled her eyes. "Lorna was in her right mind. But leaving everything to me makes me want to reconsider."

"Or maybe she knew you possessed all the traits to handle this kind of money. You're a hard worker. You're kind. You're everything her family isn't. Didn't you say she often thought of you as a granddaughter?" Rhode asked.

Teegan nodded. "I need a cup of tea."

"And we need to change all the locks on these doors. I don't trust her family. They weren't making idle threats. And I have to wonder if she was killed because they didn't realize she'd already amended the will and wanted it to stay the same. Misty might have been in the wrong place at the wrong time and had to die differently to throw off law enforcement."

Teegan couldn't imagine that, but money had motivated many murders. "You think one of the Landoons murdered Lorna for the money and my sister was a casualty?"

Rhode handed her the papers. "I think it's possible. And if you're dead, contesting the will becomes a lot easier."

After the reading of the will, the suspect pool had skyrocketed. The amount of money Teegan had inherited was easily enough motivation to kill her. More than Rhode would make in several lifetimes. The kind of dough that would catapult him from debt and pay off all his mom's medical bills. And then some.

But money didn't solve all problems. Sometimes money made things worse.

After everyone had made their dramatic exits earlier today, Rhode had first called Dom to inform him of the situation. Dom was looking into Evangeline, Glen, Charlie, Dexter and Peter Landoon. Next, he'd had a locksmith come out to change all the locks. Teegan had agreed to install a security system, but they couldn't come out until Monday morning. Rhode only wished he could have been the one to foot the bill for all this, but about all he could afford was a doorbell camera. It had hit him then: what would Teegan need him for now? She had everything—security, stability, and a massive estate for the babies to grow up on. What could he realistically bring to the table? Offering meager child support was now laughable.

And Teegan had the funds that Rhode didn't, which meant if she didn't want Rhode to see the children, she could hire fancy lawyers and take him to court and win. She'd never mentioned he wasn't going to be allowed to see the children, and had welcomed his help. But then, she hadn't known about his alcoholism. That knowledge might change her mind.

A pit formed in his gut as he climbed the stairs to check in on Teegan. She'd skipped lunch in favor of a nap. That was a few hours ago. It was now four o'clock. Maybe she'd have the elevator fixed too; these stairs were steep and many.

Rhode knocked on her bedroom door.

No answer.

He knocked harder and called her name. A shuffling noise met his ears and then the door opened. Teegan's eyes were puffy and her hair in disarray. A jagged line creased her cheek from her pillow.

"Hey, I'm sorry to wake you, but you haven't eaten, and I thought you might want a bite and then head back to the ranch for the twins."

"Right." She rubbed her eyes and yawned. "I guess I've been sleep deprived way too long, and today has been emotionally draining. I didn't realize I'd crashed so hard. I'm sorry. I don't want your family to think I'm taking advantage."

"I've already talked to them and they're fine. You needed the rest."

"I can fix us something."

Teegan always thought of others first. "I didn't wake you up to be my chef, Teegan. I know how to cook…some things."

She raised an eyebrow. "Oh yeah? Like what?"

They descended the stairs. "Well, I can

make scrambled eggs or even an egg sandwich. Egg salad. I make a great omelet and—"

"Anything that isn't egg related?" she asked as the staircase rounded.

"I make homemade pizza and tacos. I can grill a mean steak and bake a potato."

She paused near the bottom of the stairs, staring at the place she found her sister and Lorna.

"Hey. Hey," he said again, and she finally looked at him. Her face was pale and her bottom lip quivered. "It's going to be okay." He prayed he wasn't giving her false hope.

With no leads, anyone could be the murderer.

"I don't know that it is. In fact, I fear it could be even worse. I've taken what the Landoon family should have and been threatened. I've been attacked. I don't understand why or by who. My sister and Lorna are dead. And I'm constantly feeling watched. In fact, I woke up once and it was like someone was in my room. But I didn't see anyone."

She undid her ponytail holder and pulled her hair back, twisting it into a messy bun on top of her head as they walked into the massive kitchen.

Now Teegan's kitchen. If she would even want to stay in this place after what she'd endured.

"I'm going to make us some dinner. Pizza, if the ingredients are here, and we'll just take it minute by minute."

Teegan glanced around the kitchen as if checking to make sure they were truly safe and nodded.

"The kids are fine at the ranch."

"Are you sure? I know what little terrors they are." Love filled every syllable.

"Are you kidding me? They're loving it. Sissy used to babysit for free. Stone had to remind her it was a job and she was to ask for money, but she loved babies so much, she didn't feel right about asking or taking payment. Mama told him to leave her alone, but Stone hounded her until she asked Mrs. Freezy for ten dollars, then cried and returned it."

Teegan snorted. "Sissy is sweet."

"Sissy's a sucker." He smirked and opened the fridge. Well stocked, it appeared to have what they'd need for pizza. Rhode washed his hands and went to work making dough and stealing glances at Teegan. She had every reason to feel on edge, but he had hoped his presence might calm her some.

After letting the pizza dough rest, he then went to work on the homemade sauce and browning Italian sausage. The kitchen smelled amazing. Basil, garlic, onions and tomatoes with that delicious yeast dough. But Teegan didn't appear to have an appetite. Her knee bobbed and she continued scraping her hands on her thighs.

Rhode popped the pizza in the oven and walked to her. "Hey, I know you're scared and us making dinner isn't going to change what happened, but I need you to eat when this timer beeps and keep up your strength. I'm going to protect you, Teegan. And our children."

"I'm going to go wash my face and pray. I'll be right back." She left the kitchen and Rhode leaned against the counter, letting his mind work out the puzzle pieces they had at the moment. Barely a few edge pieces. He rubbed his shoulders just as a shriek filled the air.

Teegan.

Rhode raced up the stairs and met a shaking Teegan at the top. "What is it?"

She pointed to her room. "My bed. It's on my bed!"

Rhode didn't waste any time. He bolted past her and into her room. Curled on one of the pillows was a bloody snake. A note had been nailed into the middle of the body.

Grabbing a tissue box from the end table, he poked the snake to make sure it was dead. It was a rattler and deadly if alive. Once he was sure it was dead, he lifted the note with a tissue and read the bright red letters.

Snakes die!

Teegan stood in the doorway, eyes wide and her arms wrapped around her middle as if trying to shield herself from this nightmare.

"I don't know if it's safe for me and the children to be here." Her voice cracked and popped with each word. "Do you?"

"Honesty?"

"I'm not a fan of lies."

That was why he had to find a way to tell her about himself before she found out on her own. She'd assume he was deceiving her. He wasn't. He was just scared he'd lose his kids before he ever truly had them. "I'm not sure you're safe anywhere. You own millions—"

"I never asked for that. I don't think I want that kind of money. I mean, I'm honored Lorna would think me to be responsible enough for this, but I don't want a family tearing each other apart because of me. I'm not a snake. I didn't try and finagle an inheritance from Lorna. It's obvious one of the family members did this. But how? How did they get inside the house? I wasn't imagining someone in my room watching me. Someone was!"

He planned to investigate that immediately. "Teegan, the Landoon family has been fractured for a long time and they'll find a way to shred each other regardless. Lorna wanted you to have it. Anyone with a brain knows you're not a snake. Did you read the letter she left you?"

Lorna had included a personal letter for Teegan.

She nodded. "Before I fell asleep. I was going to talk to you about it. Rhode, I think there's a legit treasure."

If that was true it explained the lengths this person was going to in order to rid the world of Teegan—and Lorna for that matter.

"Let me read it to you." She opened her nightstand drawer and pulled out a piece of paper.

"Hey, why didn't Lorna fix the elevator?"

"She never went past ground level."

And that was another thing bothering Rhode. If a ninety-two-year-old woman never went upstairs, how had she gotten up there to have fallen?

Dom had said the autopsy report showed she'd died from blunt force trauma and the medical examiner had ruled it an accident. She'd also broken several bones, including both hip bones, but the head wound had immediately killed her. Guess God was merciful in that—she'd never felt her body break.

Her manner of death hadn't explained why she'd been on the second floor, though. Rhode and his brothers had discovered traces of blood on the side of the banister.

What if Lorna's death wasn't an accident, especially if there had been a treasure? He'd told Teegan he would take the case, and he'd meant it. Beau was already looking into the family members. They all had motive, but who had the most motive or the guts to murder two people in cold blood?

Teegan unfolded the letter with shaky fingers and began reading.

"My dearest Teegan,
How you have brought me such joy. You've been a treasure to me—one that is in front of me and yet buried deep within my heart. You, more than anyone, deserve what I've given you.

I know you'll steward it well. I hope it will give you the relief you need to go back to local theater and help teach young people how to love the art, but also to recognize it's not fame they should long for but God. Help them use their talent for the Lord and not for themselves.

Speaking of treasure, it's raining outside, but my heart is warm with sparkling delight. Let's drink to the occasion, love.

Sincerely,
Lorna"

Teegan lowered the letter. "She used the word *treasure* twice. The rest is a little cryptic, but I think there's a clue in it. I also think I was given this privately because it's so cryptic, it sounds like she's out of her gourd. I need to talk to Sylvia—the senior attorney who visited often."

"Maybe she'll tell us who the beneficiaries of the previous will were." That would help them with their suspect list. "Read the letter again."

She did. "I'm not sure what it means, but because it's so weird—and she uses *treasure* twice, as if for emphasis—it makes me think she's talking in code to me. I'll chew on it."

"That reminds me, I need to check the pizza and get rid of this." He dumped the snake in the bathroom trash and carried it downstairs. Rhode threw it out back but kept the note. "You got a plastic bag?"

"Yeah." She retrieved one and handed it to him. He tucked it with the tissue into the bag as evidence to give to Dom.

The oven beeped and he removed the pizza.

"It's nice on the patio. You want to eat outside?" she asked. "I'll try to eat but I'm not making any promises."

He nodded, and they carried their plates, napkins and drinks to the outdoor table. The pergola over their heads had been woven with multicolored lights, and the air was crisp.

"I love Christmastime," Rhode said, hoping to lighten the moment so she could stomach the food.

"I do too. I bought the kids so much, it's ridiculous. I have to wrap it all, and I kinda dread it." She laughed and nibbled her pizza while Rhode wondered which family member had been in the house and how they got inside her room with that snake.

Not to mention the death threat that came along with the dead creature. *Snakes die.*

The peal of a car alarm snapped his attention to the front of the house and away from his thoughts.

"That's my car," Teegan said, dropping her pizza on the plate.

"Stay here." Rhode jumped up, pulled his gun from his holster and raced through the house and out the front door.

FIVE

Teegan braced herself at the kitchen island, her fingers trembling. A bird flying into the windshield could have set off the alarm. But too much had happened in the past twenty-four hours to believe that. What if Rhode had been ambushed?

Teegan crept through the kitchen toward the foyer, the car alarm's shrill growing louder. She peeked out the front door. Rhode stood in front of the vehicle with his gun in hand, darting his sight around the lawn. Snagging her keys off the side table by the front door she stepped onto the porch and hit the button.

Silence permeated the air and Rhode pivoted in her direction.

That's when she saw it.

Her car.

Painted on the side in white: *You're Dead!*

Teegan's heart lurched into her throat, tightening it. This had now gone from a cryptic and terrifying message to making it clear. She was the snake. And she was dead. She licked her bottom lip and worked to breathe. "Did you see who did it?"

Rhode shook his head. "They're gone."

Teegan was certain this claim was a promise, one someone had already tried to make good on. "What if I gave the money back and the estate? I mean… I don't need it. I'm doing okay on my own and the kids are healthy and happy. If I don't give them what they want, I could end up like Misty. And my kids…what would happen to them? I'm all they have."

Rhode's face crumpled and he ate up the ground between them. He gently gripped her shoulders. "We are not going to let them scare you into doing what they want. And… you're not all they have now. They have me too. I want to be a part of their lives. I won't let anything happen to you, Teegan. You have my word."

Teegan barely knew Rhode. How could she trust his word? Yet, deep in the marrow of her bones, she believed she could. She weakly nodded. "Now what?"

"Now we lock up and go to the ranch."

"Should we come back at all?"

Rhode's lips twisted to the side and his brow furrowed. He was quiet a few moments then nodded. "If they're serious about coming after you, then they're going to do it no matter where you are. I say show them you aren't scared—"

"Except I am. I am scared, Rhode. My sister is dead. Lorna is dead. This is no joke. I can't take chances. I have to do what is safest for my children." Teegan couldn't care less about showing a brave front. All she cared about was staying alive and protecting the twins.

"I know. I'm not saying this to use you as bait or to antagonize them. This is your home. For as long as you want it. I'll stay here with you."

"Okay, I trust you."

Twenty minutes later, they barreled down the dark backroads to his ranch.

"You give any more thought to that letter you think is about hidden treasure?" Rhode asked. "You've been quiet."

She had a lot to think about. "It's teetering on the edge of my memory, but nothing is clear. Not yet. It's the last line that's cryptic and why I think she's telling me something without outright telling me."

It's raining outside, but my heart is warm with sparkling delight. Let's drink to the occasion, love.

Teegan pictured Lorna writing it in her shaky but gorgeous penmanship. "Let's drink to the occasion" made no sense. Lorna knew how Teegan felt about alcohol and Lorna only had red wine once a week for the antioxidants. "Lorna would never suggest a drink with her for any occasion. Lorna knows my whole story and never judged. I really am going to miss her, and my sister. I wish we'd been closer."

Rhode reached over and clasped her hand. "I know."

After pulling into the drive, Rhode grabbed a bag from the back seat. The air was crisp and the moon was full, but it didn't feel romantic. No, it was like an ominous spotlight on her, revealing her position to an unseen enemy.

Christmas might be coming. But so was a killer.

She shuddered and they entered the warm ranch. The scent of cinnamon and vanilla enveloped her senses before being met with the aroma of fresh coffee. She hoped it was decaf.

River was engaged in building a huge tower of blocks in the living room with help from Stone. Bridge was playing peek-a-boo with Brook's big pink brick. Brook's giggles were infectious.

Rhode leaned down to Teegan's ear. "Bridge is mush when it comes to babies and kids. Stone, on the other hand, is more about making sure River—at barely two—understands architecture."

"And where do you land when it comes to kids?" she asked.

He grinned. "I'm Mrs. Doubtfire meets Indiana Jones."

She laughed and it drew the attention of the twins and Rhode's brothers. Brook tottered toward her, River right behind calling, "Ma-ma. Ma-ma."

She scooped up each baby in an arm and kissed them. "Have you been good?"

"They're awesome," Bridge said. "Super smart. So it's obvious that comes from you."

Teegan laughed at his teasing.

"River could be a great architect one day," Stone said.

"Told ya," Rhode said under his breath. "Where's everybody else?" he asked his brothers.

Stone stood and stretched. "Mama went to lie down awhile. She let the babies help make cookies, so that was a disaster, and then she cooked dinner to keep Emily from the kitchen. We wanted to actually enjoy the meal."

"That woman is super, but she is the

worst cook on the planet, and that's including me," Bridge said.

"Preach," Stone said through a chuckle. "Anyway, Mama said she'd be recharged in about an hour." His eyes softened. "Rhode, she had the best time with these babies. I haven't seen her that lit up in a long time."

Bridge agreed. "He's right. She was so alive tonight. Thank you for letting the babies stay, Teegan. They're good medicine for us all."

Teegan's heart warmed and she looked around. "Where's Emily now?"

"Had to go into work. Case came up," Stone said.

"She works for the Texas Ranger's Public Integrity Unit, right?" Teegan asked.

Stone nodded. "Beau and Sissy will be here—"

The back door opened and Sissy's two adorable Cavalier King Charles spaniels bounded into the living room. The babies squirmed to get down, so Teegan complied and the dogs licked their cheeks. "Play nice with the puppies." River could grab their hair too tight. They were good sports but children needed to be taught how to respect animals so they didn't hurt them or end up nipped themselves.

"Teegan," Sissy said, "how are you feeling after the big news?" She pointed to her husband and Rhode's business partner. "Beau told me about the case."

Beau's bright blue eyes met Teegan's with compassion. "I'm looking into the bluebonnets left behind at the scene and into Misty's life in California. I am sorry for your loss. Miss Landoon was a wonderful person. I always enjoyed it when I had the chance to see her."

Teegan appreciated his sentiment. "Thank you. Have you found anything?" She glanced at the babies to ensure they were playing nicely with the Cavaliers.

Beau glanced at Rhode and then back to Teegan. "Misty had been working as a receptionist for a dental office. She was let go and charged for stealing pain meds and coming into work intoxicated. A neighbor lady told me that she'd been doing well prior to that incident and had been sober for almost three months. But she had a bad breakup with a man named Kenny Lee—we're tracking him down."

Rhode winced and Teegan's shoulders tightened. She and her sister had gone in two different directions. Teegan refusing to touch anything that might enslave her—sans the one night. Misty had gone down the road their mom had traveled.

"Do you believe this Kenny Lee came from California to Texas, targeting Misty?" Rhode asked.

"I'm not sure, but it's a lead worth tracking." Beau massaged the back of his tanned neck. "According to the neighbor, Kenny Lee was no good. Misty didn't make good choices in men and when it didn't end well, instead of being thankful, she tanked it all."

"What kind of no good?" Teegan asked.

"She'd heard fights and things breaking inside Misty's apartment before. She called the police three different times and noticed bruises on Misty. Misty denied the abuse. Made up lame excuses," Beau said.

"Who broke off the relationship?" Teegan asked.

"Misty. But it was reluctant, and Kenny didn't take it well. That's why I'm trying to track him down. Revenge is a strong motivator."

Beau was right about that. "Why continue coming after me? If he knows he killed Misty then it should be over. Right?"

Beau sighed. "I thought about that."

"And?" Rhode asked.

"She might be a reminder. He could think you're actually Misty pretending to be the sister and so he's bent on taking you both out. Or…or a family member is using her death to orchestrate yours so that we'll think the same person—possibly Kenny— is the cause of Lorna and Misty's deaths as well as yours."

Rhode rubbed his chin. "Did Misty have ties to bluebonnet flowers? And have you heard from Dom?" he asked Beau. "He was running the signature through VICAP."

"Not yet. He said he'd call as soon as he hears something."

River rubbed his eyes and yawned. The family had tuckered him out. Teegan was exhausted too. Rhode squatted and stroked River's chubby cheek. "You tired, bud?" He held out his arms and River reached for him. Rhode scooped him up and laid his nose to River's sweet button nose. "Do you like to rock?"

"He does," Teegan whispered as a lump grew in her throat. Seeing River with his father tugged her in deep places. "It's their bedtime for sure. I wish they could be in their home."

"We can go back, Teegan. I know you packed everything up this morning, but I don't believe geography is the problem."

She nodded. "You're right." She was going to be afraid no matter where she slept. Her kids needed routine and if she were being honest, so did she.

He pointed to the kitchen. "I left our pizza we didn't get to finish on the counter. Dig in."

Teegan wasn't hungry but knew she needed to eat. She and Sissy headed for the kitchen, but River and Brook had crawled into Rhode's lap in the rocking chair. Marisol woke from her evening nap and the house was full of chatter and laughter. For now, it felt like a normal family.

Although she wasn't sure what normal was. Teegan had never been a part of people who razzed each other, laughed together and clearly loved one another. She was happy her children had a large family of people who adored them.

But Teegan was on the outside. She and Rhode weren't together. Weren't married. And, while she was attracted to him and they got along, it didn't mean family.

She was on her own. As she always had been.

Rhode stretched his arms over his head and yawned. "I'm glad you had a portable crib for the babies. The other one is a beast." After leaving his family's ranch, with sleeping babies, they'd carried them upstairs and put them in their portable crib, snoozing soundly. "My family is exhausting. Even for babies," Rhode teased through a whisper.

Teegan smiled and turned on the monitor then clipped the receiver on her waist. Nothing but the sound of static and baby breaths.

"I've been thinking about that letter."

"What did you come up with?"

"Let's go to Lorna's theater room. I have a suspicion." They descended the stairs and marched to the back of the home where Lorna's theater room housed leather recliners with cup holders, red-velvet curtains flanking a massive movie screen, and a projector booth at the back of the room. It even had a popcorn and drink machine at a bar in the right corner. "Lorna loved movies and often had friends come to watch a flick. But she especially loved her own movies and often watched them. I've seen them all, but some more than others. I believe that last sentence in my letter is a line from one of her movies."

Teegan headed for the projector booth.

"She won an Oscar for her role as Miriam Malone in the 1953 hit *A Love Affair in Venice*. She starred opposite Cary Grant. They did several movies together. Their on-screen chemistry was dynamic."

"I haven't seen it. I'm not an old movie buff, but Sissy loves them. She said she'd seen all of Lorna's movies too."

The projector rolled and the film began.

"There's a part when Cary is leaving her to return to the States and the affair is over. He mentioned his wife traveled overseas and encountered a shipwreck. He traveled to Venice to mourn the loss and meets Miriam Malone, who bought a vineyard and small hotel. It was a whirlwind romance. But then he gets word that they have found his wife. She's not dead. But Miriam has captured his heart, and now he's torn."

"That's awful."

Teegan nodded. "It devastated me. But Miriam makes it easy on him and tells him to return to his first love. She sends him off with a bottle of wine they cultivated together. It was this emotional scene that won her the Oscar. I cry every time I watch it. It's heart-wrenching."

They watched in silence. Halfway through, Teegan pointed to the screen. "This is the scene in the wine cellar."

Lorna was a stunner. Her ruby-red lips and teary eyes drew Rhode in.

Cary Grant cradled her face. "I can't leave you, darling. I love you. You've healed me and brought me back to life. A life I didn't want to live. And now, I don't want to live it without you."

Lorna touched his cheek, her long lashes damp with tears. "You must go back. She needs you. And you'll find you need her."

Thunder cracked and the sound of rain erupted. She paused among the rows of wine. "I met you in the rain."

"I kissed you in the rain."

Lorna broke free and closed her eyes. "How you have brought me such joy. It's raining outside, but my heart is warm with sparkling delight. Let's drink to the occasion, love. One last drink." She opened a bottle of wine and poured two glasses. They drank it through tears and then she handed him a bottle. "Always remember me."

Cary held the wine bottle. "I could never forget you. I wouldn't want to. Oh, darling." He grabbed her with intensity and kissed her passionately, then left without looking back, the bottle of wine in hand.

Teegan wiped her eyes. "She was a fabulous actress. But I think she's giving us a clue. When she had the house built, it included a cellar. In fact, a lot of what Lorna has around her estate is from movies. She aspired to be done with that life, but the acting in itself she never stopped loving or missing."

"Will the baby monitor work in the wine cellar?"

"Yep."

Rhode motioned for her to lead the way. At the back of the house, a door opened to old wooden stairs and the temperature plummeted. Teegan switched on the light at the top and they descended slowly, Teegan leading the way.

Rows and rows of large shelves held bottles of wines. So much wine, one would never drink it in a lifetime. Rhode felt the dry ache in his throat and cleared it.

"You okay?" Teegan asked.

"Yeah." He said a silent prayer for strength. The scent of fermentation and grapes filled his senses as the memories of the dry, fruity drink hit him like a gut punch. Like Joseph, he needed to flee. "Actually, I'm not feeling well all of a sudden. I need some air. Do you mind if I wait upstairs?"

She paused and studied him.

Rhode should take the moment to confess the truth and that he was tempted to have a drink. He regretted the current situation and wished he'd have no taste for it anymore. He longed for the struggle to end. Embarrassment coupled with weakness and knowledge of Teegan's opinion on those who imbibed cemented his tongue to the roof of his mouth.

"Are you claustrophobic?" she asked with a smirk.

Right now, in this moment? "Yes," he answered honestly. The walls were closing in on him and he might have a panic attack.

"Go on. I'm pretty sure I know what I'm looking for."

He sighed. "Thank you." He rushed back up the stairs, closing the door behind him, and beelined it straight for the kitchen where he turned on the faucet and splashed his face with cold water. Would this ever go away? Would he have to run away like a coward every time he desired a taste? Frustration knotted his shoulders and neck muscles, and he squeezed his eyes closed.

Hairs on his neck prickled and he spun around just in time to see a man looming over him, a creepy white jester mask with an insidious red grin and black diamonds painted around the eyes.

Rhode reached back to waylay him, but the jester got the jump on him, clobbering him with something hard.

Those black diamonds around his eyes were the last thing Rhode saw before he drifted into his own blackness.

SIX

Teegan sneezed as dust and cobwebs tickled her nose. The dim light concentrated on the stairs, shadows branching out before them onto the concrete flooring. Must and the scent of fermentation permeated the cellar.

She hoped Rhode was okay and not too overwhelmed, but she wondered if it might be more than that. Something felt off. She'd honed the knack for sensing when a person was withholding information. She'd had to since it had been just her and Misty since childhood.

Oh, Miss.

Teegan had tried dozens of times to prompt her twin to move back. She'd had it in her head that while she couldn't fix their mother, she could Misty. That wasn't true though. The reality was that a person couldn't help another person who didn't want help, or she'd have seen her mom make progress. She never had and she'd drank herself to death.

Teegan studied the dusty wine bottles, some worth thousands of dollars. Crazy how a fermented grape could go for twelve grand. In the movie, they had held a dark green bottle with a purple cork. The wines were in order of year and she was looking for 1953—the year the movie had been released.

There was 1956...54...

Boom!

Excitement built in her chest and she wished Rhode was down here to share this moment. Was that weird? She slipped the bottle from the wooden holder.

An empty bottle, but the one from the set. It had probably been filled with grape juice.

Teegan popped the cork and found a rolled-up white paper inside.

The next clue!

Heavy, slow footsteps clunked on the wooden stairs.

Rhode had overcome his fear.

"Rhode. I found it. I was right!"

Rhode didn't respond and her scalp tingled as the chilly air swirled around her. "Rhode," she whispered, her throat tight.

The footsteps silenced.

Teegan shifted but couldn't see past the looming shadows peeking out from the corners. The rows of wooden shelves blocked her vision.

She gripped the wine bottle and shoved the rolled-up clue into her waistband. She tiptoed to the end of the row with her back flush to the end cap. Her heart hammered against her ribs and she covered her mouth to keep from gasping.

Rhode wasn't down here with her.

But someone was.

If she screamed, would he hear her? Whoever was in the cellar with her definitely would and she'd give away her position. It was a matter of time before he found her anyway.

Shuffling along the concrete ignited a jolt through her system and her fight-or-flight kicked in. She bolted from the shelves just in time to bounce into a large frame dressed in black.

The terrifying jester mask with the wicked smile painted in ruby-red stared at her. In his gloved hand there was a very large butcher knife, glinting in the dim light.

He raised it and she shrieked; the wound in her flesh where he'd already torn through throbbed. She bolted the way she'd come and rounded the shelf. He raced after her. Circling it, she aimed for the staircase. As she reached the bottom stair, he gripped the back of her hair and yanked her toward him. She stumbled and fell as the knife swooped through the air, narrowly missing her stomach. She scrambled on her hands and knees for the inner cellar. Once she was on her feet, she darted down a row of wines.

Creaking and groaning gave her pause, then she pivoted as the shelves shuddered then toppled over, bottles crashing to the floor and scattering glass shards across the red-stained concrete. Like blood, the wine oozed and pooled at her feet.

She screamed again as another row crashed down, clipping her back and forcing her to drop to the floor, pinning her. Agonizing pain shot up her right leg to her head as it smacked against the bottom of a rack, the bottles falling like dominoes in front of her.

The jester loomed over her; the knife blade glittering. She raised her hands in defense and shrieked, "Please don't. I have babies. Please!"

"Teegan!" Rhode thundered.

"Rhode!"

Pain blinded her. Spots dotted her vision as the last thing she saw was the shiny, bloodstained knife raised above her head and heard the words of the jester.

"…gets…last…now…"

"You're okay. Stay still," Rhode said. He pushed the wooden wine shelf from her leg. "Can you move it?"

"Where is he? Where are my babies?" How long had she been out? She was alive!

Rhode held up the monitor. "They're fine. But if you can move, I want to check on them."

She nodded and moved her leg, wincing. "It's not broken, but it hurts. Where did he go?"

"He was gone when I got down here. Maybe three, four minutes ago. Is there a cellar door that leads outside?"

Teegan pointed to the east side of the room and Rhode raced to it. "It's locked. How did he escape then?"

"I'm not sure," she said through the pain. Every muscle in her body ached and her head pounded. "I want to stand. Want to see my babies."

Rhode helped her to her feet; her ankle smarted. Relief flooded her when she could put weight on her foot. Not broken. Bruised for sure. "What happened to you?"

"He came into the kitchen and got the jump on me. Knocked me out. I'm so sorry. I said I'd protect you and I failed,

Teegan." His voice was low and full of disappointment.

"Rhode, you couldn't have known. How did he even get in the house? The doors were locked."

"I don't know. Can you make it upstairs?"

"I don't know."

"Can I have permission to carry you?" he asked.

How embarrassing. But she wanted to be close to the babies. "Okay."

He swept her up as if she weighed nothing and climbed the stairs. "You're shaking," he said. "I'm so sorry."

"You saved me. He was going to kill me, Rhode. Right before I blacked out, he said something, but I couldn't hear it all. His voice was fuzzy in my ears. I did make out three words. *Gets. Last. Now.* What does that mean?"

"I don't know." He reached the top of the stairs and eased her onto the couch in the loft then covered her with a blanket. He checked the babies' room and returned. "All is well in there. Stay here and I'll clear the house." He drew a small can from his pocket. "Pepper spray. It shoots thirty feet. You spray and move. He'll be blinded and unable to tell where you moved to."

Gripping the can, she nodded, and Rhode began clearing the second floor then went downstairs.

Which one of the family members would be this vicious? This cold-blooded? The money, the home and estate weren't worth this. Not even a little.

Finally, Rhode returned. "It's all clear, and I called Dom again. Told him the jester wore gloves, but he's sending the crime scene techs anyway. Be about thirty minutes." He slumped next to her and searched her eyes. "How are you feeling?" He lightly touched a cut on her cheek and she winced. "Let me fix you up." He stood and helped her to the bathroom.

"Sit," he ordered, and she sat on the toilet lid. He opened the medicine cabinet and retrieved hydrogen peroxide. He found a rag and ran it under warm water.

"I can do this myself, Rhode." But her hands wouldn't stop trembling.

"I know." He knelt in front of her and held her hands until the warmth of his steadied her. "It'll be boo-boo fixer practice for the kids."

She actually smiled. "My dad wasn't around to fix boo-boos."

He held her gaze and she inhaled the subtle scent of his cologne that lingered on his clothing, which evoked a sweeping memory of dancing in his arms, even though his face was fuzzy.

"I'm not going anywhere, Teegan," he whispered. "Maybe your dad told you the same thing. I don't know. But I'm here. I'm going to be the dad those babies deserve to the best of my ability, but I'll be honest, I don't have much in the way of money. I do have love and all of myself. And anything I do have is theirs."

Tears washed over her eyes and she bit her bottom lip to tamp down the sobs. Her dad had never said he'd stay. Never said much at all. "I believe you."

He applied the warm washcloth to her cheek, dabbing delicately, and brushed a stray hair stuck to her skin before slipping it behind her ear. "I don't remember that night, but I must have been knocked for a loop by you. You're...so beautiful." His finger trailed her jawline. "So sweet."

Teegan's chest fractured, the ache painful but thrilling. He poured the peroxide on the rag and pressed it to the abrasion, holding it in place while arresting her gaze and maybe...just maybe...cuffing her heart.

No. She couldn't let that happen. A few compliments didn't equal commitment. And even if it did, she'd been committed to and left before. By family. By her fiancé. She couldn't be crippled emotionally again.

"I have the clue," she said instead, snuffing out the flame that had been flickering between them. She pulled the slip of paper from her waistband.

"Where did you find it?" Rhode removed the rag and stood, rinsing it out and hanging it on the towel rack then examining his reflection—and the goose egg—in the mirror. They both needed an ice pack.

"In a stage prop wine bottle."

He frowned at his face in the mirror and she had a feeling he was beating himself up for being caught off guard. "What's it say?"

"'Oh, how I can make an entrance. I'm a showstopper, darling.'" Teegan frowned and turned the paper over. Blank. One line.

"Do you know what movie that's from?"

"Not off hand." Disappointment dropped heavy in her stomach. "Do you have your phone?"

He nodded.

"Can you Google it?"

Rhode pulled his phone from his pocket and googled the line. His lips turned downward. "Nothing."

Teegan sighed. She had hoped it would be as easy as the first clue.

Nothing was easy. Story of her life.

She wouldn't give up though. Teegan had never been a quitter. "I'll figure it out. I may have to sift through some of her movies."

"*We'll* figure it out. For now, let's wait on the forensic team and then try to sleep."

Rhode was right. There wasn't more she could do tonight. She'd fall dead asleep if she turned on a movie. Her limbs felt like lead and her brain was foggy. Teegan needed rest and pain relievers. The babies would wake and be full of energy regardless of her exhaustion and aching body.

But they'd found the clue. Lorna wanted them to find something greater.

What treasure could be as great as what Lorna had already left her?

Rhode's eyes cracked open when one of the babies cried through the monitor. Last night, after the forensic team had left, Rhode had taken the baby monitor from Teegan and persuaded her to hit the hay for uninterrupted sleep. He glanced at his cell phone. Way too early to be awake, but he rolled off the couch in the loft area and rubbed his eyes as he padded to the nursery. He hoped they'd be okay with seeing him and not their mama. They might not be timid around strangers but they were used to seeing their mama in the mornings. Not him.

He cracked open the door and Brook stood in the portable crib, her little hands wrapping over the top. River slept through her whimpers. When he was younger, Rhode could sleep through a bomb too. "Hi, baby girl," he whispered. "It's Daddy." He hoped Teegan didn't mind, but he was their father and he wanted them to know it. Brook shied away and a pang hit his gut. "It's okay, baby girl. Come on." Holding out his arms, he waited until she reached for him and allowed him to lift her from the crib. The act melted him into a puddle of slush. River slept soundly, his little chest rising and falling rhythmically.

Rhode grabbed a diaper and wipes then slipped from the room. In the loft, he laid her on the couch and changed her wet diaper then sat her on his lap. "You feel better now?"

She rubbed her sleepy eyes and grabbed at his hair.

"Yeah, we got a lot of it, kiddo." He kissed her forehead.

"Juice."

"Okay, princess, let's get you some juice." He was about to clip the monitor to his waist when he heard River.

"Ma-ma. Ma-ma!" No cries, just demands.

"Let's take bubba with us, okay?" He hurried into the room where River stood, banging a dinosaur on the crib. A fat grin filled his face when he saw Rhode and Brook.

"Hey, bud." He put Brook down and picked up River, taking him to the changing table. "I thought you were gonna sleep all day." He kissed his cheek and changed his diaper. "You want juice too?"

"Juice."

"I hear ya, bruh." He put him on his hip, snatching Brook back up, and carried them down the stairs. "Y'all are work. No wonder Mama is still asleep."

"Ma-ma," Brook said.

"I know you want Mama. She's going night-night." Once he arrived in the kitchen, he buckled them into high chairs and went to work hunting down sippy cups and pouring apple juice. "You hungry?"

"Hun-gy," Brook said as she accepted the cup.

Rhode pulled eggs and butter from the fridge and a loaf of bread off the counter for scrambled eggs and toast.

By the time River dumped his eggs and Brook had eaten most of her toast, Teegan entered the kitchen. "I can't believe I slept this late."

He held up the pan. "You hungry? I think I got a second round of eggs and toast in me."

She nodded and spoke to the babies, kissing heads that had eggs and toast smooshed in their hair. "Thank you." Her eyes pooled and Rhode laid the spatula on the counter and closed the distance between them.

"What's wrong?"

"I just... I haven't slept in for almost two years, and I'm overwhelmed at your kindness."

His heart cracked. How exhausting it must be to do this day in and out alone. Single moms deserved the world. Rhode had only managed wake-up time and breakfast, and he was whipped. He'd picked up sippy cups and baby forks ten-thousand times. "Well, I'm here now. You don't have to do this alone, and while you haven't said I can't be involved, you haven't made it clear that I can."

Teegan poured a cup of coffee and sipped. "Rhode, I want you to be in your children's lives if you want to be. And by that, I mean fully and wholeheartedly in their lives. No walking out when it's tough. No neglecting them. My dad walked out when we were little, and it was devastating. My mom was an alcoholic and I can't even begin to describe what that was like for us. They need stability and security. Can you provide that for them?"

His dry throat ached. He was a recovering alcoholic. He had no plans to return to the drink. But he imagined her mother had said the same things before falling prey to the false soothing effects liquor brought. If he admitted he had the same problem,

Teegan would never allow him to be a part of the twins' lives. Yeah, he could take her to court, but she had a strong case and the funds to hire power attorneys who could tie him up in legal fees he'd never dig out from.

But she deserved to know the whole truth. And he would tell her. He would. Once she saw how great of a dad he could be.

"I won't tell you I'm some superhero, Teegan. I assure you, I have faults. I've made mistakes and I have a past I'm not proud of. But I want to be a full-time dad." He meant every single word.

"We all have a past. You know the things I'm not proud of. And if you want to be a father, I want you to be. They need one. I know what it's like to long for both parents. My dad walked out. My mom…she tried. She did. She'd get sober for a few months. Once, for a whole year, and I thought 'now things will be right.' She was present and active in our lives and then she lost her job due to budget cuts and it sent her into a tailspin. It was like she died after that, and it crushed me and Misty."

"I'm sorry," Rhode said. "Alcohol makes people act in ways they normally wouldn't."

"We both know that. I'm glad it was just a one-time mistake for us."

He swallowed hard. "But we have the babies and they're perfect."

She nodded and sipped her hot caffeine. "That, they are. Except for when they're being complete terrors." She laughed and put the coffee cup on the counter. "So what's the plan for today?"

"Well, Beau is still running down leads on Misty in California, and Dom is working the case here. I want to stay close to you—professionally, of course."

Her smile was tight. "Of course."

"But later this evening, we're putting up the tree. We used to do it on Christmas Eve, but the past two years we've done it early—the week before. And we open one gift each then watch *A Christmas Carol* and Sissy and Mama bake cookies. Us boys aren't allowed because we're terrible at it. It's pretty much a loud and obnoxious hoopla but it's our thing. I'd love for you and the twins to be there."

Teegan's eyes lit up. "I would love that, but I have no idea what to buy your family. I barely know them."

"No one will expect you to bring gifts, Teegan. But I have some shopping to do for the kiddos."

"Okay then. Later today, I need to watch some of Lorna's old movies and see if we can figure out which movie that last clue is from. I wonder how many clues there are."

"With Lorna, who knows?"

Teegan nodded. "If you're good with the babies, I'd like to walk down to the stables and talk to Harry. With last night's attack in the house, he needs to know to be careful."

"I don't know that it's a good idea."

"It's not even 8:00 a.m. I won't leave the property."

Rhode frowned. "I don't love it, but you're right. Unless…do you normally go for a walk this time of day?"

"Ha. I wish."

"Okay, then you have no routine he might know about. Take the pepper spray I gave you last night; it'll make me feel better. And maybe don't go in the labyrinth. Didn't work out well when Sissy did that." She'd been attacked by a serial killer stalking her. "How do you know Harry is down there?"

"He's like clockwork. Arrives 6:30 a.m. every single day except Sunday."

Rhode couldn't hold her hostage. "Be careful. I'm going to clean up these kiddos and get them dressed. I can't promise you they'll match, but they'll be clothed and in dry diapers."

"Fair enough."

She walked out the back door and Rhode's stomach pinched. Then he looked at the twins and groaned. Eggs, toast and sticky juice covered them from head to toe. Weren't sippy cups supposed to be spill-proof? He sighed and shook his head. "Y'all are the absolute messiest."

River clapped and Brook joined in as they giggled. No way he could be irritated at that. "It's going to take all day to clean you up, you rug rats."

His cell phone rang. Beau. He answered. "Hey, man. What's going on?"

"Have you had the news on this morning?"

"I haven't even had time to brush my teeth. I have twins. You just wait. In a few months, it'll be you."

"How did you know we were pregnant? We were waiting to tell everyone at Christmas. I mean we don't know how many babies there are." His voice carried, swelling pride and joy.

"I'm a twin. We have a sense about each other, and I *wish* two babies on you. It's awesome and scary and exhausting." He laughed and Beau chuckled. "Also, maybe don't tell Sissy you both are pregnant. She might be inclined to rip your head off."

Beau laughed. "Valid. I'm down with whatever. I'm actually pulling into the driveway. I wanted to share the news in person."

"I'm heading to let you in." Rhode hung

up and unlocked the front door, welcoming Beau inside. He was dressed in his usual trendy jeans and a fitted sports coat over a white dress shirt. "Babies are in the kitchen, follow me."

When they entered the kitchen, the babies stopped banging their cups on the high chair trays long enough to see who was with Rhode.

"Dude, did you feed them or bathe them in their breakfast?"

"Both?" He shrugged and headed for the sink to wet a washcloth. "What news needs to be shared in person?"

"Where's Teegan?"

"Talking to Harry. With pepper spray and instructions not to go into the labyrinth."

"Yeah, I'd rather not go through that again." He shivered. "So... I found out a woman was murdered two days ago in Austin. Adeline James. Stabbed to death. Dom called the detective working the case. She's the same age as Teegan and they went to the same high school, but that could be coincidence. What's not a coincidence is bluebonnets left in a pool of blood, just like with Misty."

Rhode's stomach knotted. "Have you looked into the family members individually?" He scraped the food from the trays and wiped them down.

"Yeah. I found a photo of one of Lorna's great-grandchildren with our victim. It was taken about three months ago."

"Charlie?" Rhode asked.

"No. Peter."

Hmm. "Anything else?"

"Yep." Beau shot him a sheepish grin. "I sometimes have insomnia so what else am I gonna do but work?"

"I hear ya."

"Peter dated Adeline for about eight months and, according to Adeline's roommate—who happens to be a night owl— she was the one who broke things off. She said Adeline wasn't feeling it anymore. The spark was gone."

"She say how he took it?" Rhode took a fresh rag and went to work cleaning Brook.

"Not well. According to the friend, he

called her repeatedly and sent a bouquet of bluebonnets to her work."

Teegan never mentioned dating Peter or being sent flowers by him. Was there a connection? "Keep digging and let me know what turns up. I want to go with you when you talk to Peter Landoon, but I also don't want to leave Teegan alone."

"Understood." Beau stared at the babies. "If the dogs were here, they'd lick them clean. Save you some time too."

"I don't see Teegan loving that idea."

"They'd be like Roombas for messy babies. Plus, I read that dogs' tongues are cleaner than humans'."

"Why are you reading about dog tongues?"

"Insomnia?"

Rhode sniffed. "Hey…do you smell that?"

Beau inhaled. "Maybe the gardener is burning leaves."

"No one is here but Harry Doyle." He frowned and walked to the kitchen door. A plume of smoke billowed. "Beau! I think the stables may be on fire."

Teegan was out there. Rhode knew it

had been a bad idea and kicked himself for allowing it.

"Go! I'll call 9-1-1, and I got the babies. Go!"

SEVEN

Teegan rounded the second set of stables. The horses always calmed her. They were sleek and beautiful. She inhaled the scent of leather and hay, but it was mixed with smoke. She hadn't seen Harry out there yet, and he would never light something on fire with the horses nearby and dry hay that would catch quickly and spread.

As she turned, fire crackled along the roof of the stable. She opened her mouth to scream for Harry, but a gloved hand clamped her lips closed. The faint smell of cigarettes attacked her senses. Using her elbow, she rammed the man holding her hostage in the ribs and his grip released. She sprinted toward the house, refusing to look back.

Horses ran along beside her, pushing

ahead as the fire had spooked them. Had Harry let them out this early? He didn't usually. Had someone else?

Where was Harry?

Footsteps pounding on hard-packed earth let her know she needed to pick up speed. She'd never been much into exercising, and running was for crazy people, but she wished she had more cardio in her life right now. Her chin wobbled as she sped up and her legs protested by burning and threatening to buckle, but she raced for the gardens, weaving through the rows of flower beds, pots of gorgeous blooms and the fountain with benches surrounding it. She shot into the labyrinth.

The one place Rhode had told her not to go.

But she knew it well and walked it often. Taking rights was the key, but since she was moving into it backward, she needed to make lefts. Without thought, she raced down one concrete-laden aisle flanked by massive, perfectly manicured box hedges that stood nearly ten feet tall.

Teegan's heart beat out of her tight chest. "Teegan!"

Rhode. Rhode must have seen the fire from the house. She called back and hoped he'd played Marco Polo as a child. She couldn't give away her exact location, yet hollering would also give her position away to her assailant.

She turned the corner. Footsteps pounded the ground and she pushed her back flush against the hedges as a dark figure ran past her. She prayed he wouldn't backtrack and find her. After waiting a few seconds, she continued through the labyrinth. All she had to do was reach the beginning and she'd be out. If her attacker hadn't returned the way he'd come, he'd end up stuck.

Darting a glance behind her, all was clear. She pivoted and smacked into a chest, yelping.

"It's me. It's me. Are you hurt? Did you see who did it?" Rhode asked.

Siren peals echoed in the distance. Her lungs begged for breath. She nodded. "He's in here. Ran right by me."

Rhode started in the direction she pointed but she grabbed his arm. "Unless you know this puzzle, it's a death trap. You could get lost or blindsided. Or he could find his way out and you'll end up stuck."

"Not my first time in this thing, Teegan. I really wanted that treasure."

Suddenly it dawned on her. Rhode was out here with her.

"Where are the babies?" Panic pushed her words out in short pants.

"They're okay. Beau came by and is inside with them. He called the police." He took her hand. "Let's get out of here."

They returned to the kitchen where police officers—including Rhode's cousin, Dom—stood talking with Beau. Firefighters had used the side road to the stables.

"Harry." Teegan gulped in air. "I didn't see Harry. I'm worried something bad happened."

"Don't worry. We'll find him," Dom said.

Rhode led Teegan into Lorna's sitting room where the babies were being chased by Beau, his expression frazzled.

Her heartbeat slowed and peace washed over her seeing her kiddos safe and having fun amid the danger lurking outside. Danger that had almost been her ending.

"Hey," Rhode said and Beau turned.

"These kids are going to win awards in track. I'm telling you now." Beau chuckled as River and Brook ran for Teegan.

Teegan scooped them up, one in each arm. Who needed the gym and weight training when one had twins?

"Did you find him?" Beau asked.

"No." Rhode huffed. "If he's on the property, they will though. The question is why set the stables on fire?"

"I own them now," Teegan said. "Any one of the Landoons might have. They let the horses out. They didn't want them hurt. I don't know if the fire was meant to lure me out or I was in the wrong place at the wrong time."

"It's possible they were burning them down to discourage you. And then when you showed, it was convenient to take it a step further. We need to find out what happens to the estate if you die."

"She had no clause, Rhode. Nothing stating it reverts back. I need a will drawn up immediately."

Rhode agreed.

What was she supposed to do to keep her children safe? Lorna's estate didn't feel safe at all. And the security system wasn't being installed until Monday.

"Did you know an Adeline James?" Rhode asked.

Teegan frowned. Why was he bringing up an old school friend? "Yeah, but we lost track of each other a few years ago. You know how it is when lives change and people move. Last I heard she was in Dallas. Why?"

"Because she was killed and bluebonnets were left at the scene," Rhode said.

"And she dated Peter Landoon," Beau added. "What can you tell us about him?"

Peter? Peter dated Addie? This was new information.

What did it mean?

The babies squirmed to break free and she set them down. They bolted into the living room, chasing each other and giggling before River found his little bike and climbed on. Brook got on behind him and they started scooting across the floor. She was glad to have thought to bring a few of their toys to keep them busy. The rest were back at the ranch. Lorna had always gotten such a kick out the kids. Never minding their toys and the sometimes clutter.

"I didn't know about them. I don't see Peter often, but he's always been kind. You think Peter killed Addie, Lorna and my sister?"

Rhode flushed against the wall, as the kids zoomed by nearly taking out his legs. "I don't know. But the flowers left at both crime scenes and the fact they'd both been stabbed multiple times tells me it's connected. I'm unsure of Lorna. It's possible that Misty and Addie's killer couldn't bring himself to stab Lorna. He might have been too personally connected to her, as in family."

"So there's no chance Misty walked in and saw something and was killed for simply being in the house."

"I think so," Rhode said. "I'm just not sure if the killer targeted her thinking it was you or knew it was Misty."

"Or we could be missing something," Beau added, dodging the little plastic bike. "Now we have track runners and NASCAR drivers. These kids!" He laughed. "I'll keep digging."

"What should I be doing?" Other than trying to stay alive.

"Maybe Lorna's treasure hunt will turn up something vital to the investigation. Work that movie line and see if you can find the next location."

"There's a legit treasure?" Beau asked, his blue eyes brightening. "I thought that was a rumor."

"It's not," Teegan said. "We have no idea what it is, but it's obvious Lorna wanted me to find it. She left the first clue in a private letter to me."

The question was what would Lorna have

known long ago when she hid the treasure that would be relevant to the case now? Teegan wasn't sure they linked, but it did give her something to do to keep her mind off the fact she was being hunted down by a savage killer and that her children might be in danger.

And where was Harry Doyle?

The rest of the morning had been a whirlwind of activity. Rhode had met with Dom to get updates and he'd help him pick up Teegan's car, which had been repainted. He didn't go to the Cedar Springs PD much anymore—not so much due to being ostracized but out of shame.

Rhode had made amends to the people he loved and to colleagues, but he could never make up for the pain he'd caused, the disappointment and the money it had cost those he loved most. He would forever be in debt to Beau, who had paid for his rehab, and to his family for never giving up on him. For the intervention and the tough love.

But for the pain he'd inflicted on his mama—that was one he would never forgive himself for. She'd aged years during his spiral, worrying over him, and he imagined she had calluses and rug burn on her knees from the hours of devotions on his behalf. He'd never again take for granted a praying mama. Her persevering prayers and her stubborn head to not give up had been answered. He had no way to pay her back except to live in the way he knew a man of faith should live and to be the kind of father who brought his own children before the Lord on a daily basis. He'd be proud of rug burn and calluses formed in bowing before God and making intercession.

After lunch, the babies napped and Teegan watched several old movies—and googled a few to help speed up the time. While she did that, Rhode's brothers and Beau came by to discuss the case. Harry Doyle hadn't been at work this morning like usual. He said he'd felt ill and slept in. Rhode thought that sounded too convenient, but Harry had nothing to gain by setting fire to the stables. He had a job no matter who ran the business.

Initially, they believed one of the Landoon family members had known—or suspected—Lorna was going to amend her will and killed her. Stone said Lorna's fall appeared to be accidental, but everyone knew she never went upstairs. They were considering the possibility that someone had hit her on the head, carried her upstairs then thrown her down the stairs, staging it. Misty, who had arrived to surprise her sister, had entered the house and seen the display. She'd been collateral damage.

The other possibility was that the will had already been changed, and Misty had been killed under the assumption she'd been Teegan. The killer couldn't have thrown them both down the stairs. It would point back to the will.

But stabbings were personal.

One had to get up close, look their victim in the eye, and the number of stab wounds—over seventeen, not counting self-defense wounds on her hands and fore-arms—indicated rage. Very personal rage. That made sense if a family member believed Teegan was gold-digging or going to be left the estate, businesses and all the money.

Any one of the Landoons had motive and opportunity. They all had access to the house. Lorna was lax on security. But another victim who Teegan knew personally had been stabbed multiple times and Texas bluebonnets left behind at the scene.

That didn't feel like it tied to Lorna leaving the estate to Teegan.

Peter Landoon was connected to Addie and Teegan. Could Addie have known something and her death had been to shut her up? Had Peter assumed Addie and Teegan were still friends? Would he have even known they'd been friends? Rhode wanted to know more about Addie and how she tied to Teegan. For the past hour, he'd been researching everything he could on Adeline James.

She and Teegan had attended high school

together. He'd found an online yearbook with several photos of them together with two other girls. They'd belonged to the Beta club and a scholastic bowl team. Only Teegan hadn't been a cheerleader. But Misty had. Misty, however, wasn't in the same photos with Teegan and her friends. In fact, he'd only found a handful of photos of Misty and two had been with Teegan. The others were of Misty with a rougher crowd of teenagers. Rhode wasn't one to stereotype, but stereotypes were stereotypes for a reason.

Addie had worked as a receptionist at a dental office near Austin after moving from Dallas recently. She had a roommate, whom Beau had talked to earlier, and he was going to talk to her coworkers as well. Teegan said that she'd lost touch with most of her friends from school. They'd gone off to college and run around, having a good time, but she'd worked two jobs and had had to grow up fast. She hadn't had time to waste and she hadn't had the money to throw away on concerts, habitual takeout and movies.

"Hey," Teegan said as she entered the up-stairs sitting room. He'd been working in the loft area while the babies napped in the nursery. "I found it."

"The next clue?"

"Yep. It's from the 1957 film *Make a Splash* about a starlet whose last film tanks and she's humiliated and hides out on a small farm in Upstate New York while fig-uring out what to do with her life. I think the clue is hidden in the swimming pool drain."

The swimming pool drain? How would anyone put paper in a wet drain? "Are you sure?"

"I'm ninety-nine-percent certain. She says, 'Oh, how I can make an entrance. I'm a showstopper, darling.' Then she dives into the pool and, when she comes up, her man-ager hands her a towel and tells her that her movie didn't go over, and there won't be a sequel. It sets the course of the rest of the movie. It's really good. She entered the pool, and the word *stopper* makes me think of a bathtub stopper—or a drain plug."

Teegan's guess wasn't out of the realm of possibility. "Do you think Lorna did it herself? Back in the day?"

"I do. She was an avid swimmer, which is part of the reason they gave her the part. She could easily have put on scuba gear, waterproofed it, and then shoved it inside."

"What if the pool needed maintenance? It could be found."

"If she had issues with the drain. They don't drain a pool to put in new liners. It's worth the swim to find out. The pool is heated."

"I'll call Bridge. He's the scuba dude and he's already combed her stupid lake already. This will give him new satisfaction that his diving wasn't fully in vain." Rhode chuckled. Bridge would be all over this.

"Okay, but we should wait until evening when no one is around. Bridge scuba diving will call attention. I don't know where loyalties lie. I know I kept everyone on and they're thankful, but several employees

adore Evangeline and especially Charlie—
down at the stables." Teegan sighed and
pointed at the nursery. "They were super
tired. They'll be much easier to manage tonight at your ranch. Don't get me wrong,
they'll be buck-wild but less temper tan-
trums."

Rhode grinned. "My mom raised a rowdy
bunch of boys. We can handle feisty twins."

"You say that now."

The entire family was inside and as they
entered with the babies, the Christmas
"Chipmunk Song" played and he cocked
his head. "Last Christmas, this song didn't
pan out well with us."

His remark about their fun brotherly
wrestling match last year sent laughter
through the home. It was warm and cozy;
the fireplace going, though it wasn't truly
cold enough. Sissy caught his eye and
grinned. "Bridge turned on the air-condi-
tioning so we wouldn't burn up from the
fireplace heat. He said it would balance out.
Stone grumbled over electric bills."

"Sounds about right."

Teegan had Brook, and his mother and Emily were going nuts over her. Sissy snatched River from Rhode. "You going to announce your big news?" So much for letting Sissy pretend to at least surprise him.

"I should have known you knew. You havin' sympathy pains? Urinating more often? Feeling nauseous?" Sissy held River's little hand and kissed it.

"No, but I often felt that way when I was on the sauce, which…can we not bring up my issues with Teegan? I haven't told her. Hasn't been the right time." Rhode wasn't sure if it would ever be the right time. Fear had built a big, impenetrable wall between his mouth and Teegan.

"I didn't expect to be all, 'Have a holly, jolly Christmas and, oh, by the way, Rhode's a recovering alcoholic.'" She snorted then froze.

Rhode's hairs along his arm prickled and he slowly pivoted.

Standing directly behind him was Teegan.

EIGHT

Teegan must have heard wrong. It was a joke pertaining to their one night in Dallas. "Is that true?" she whispered, her throat and chest tight.

Rhode glanced at Sissy and her eyes pulsed with apology. It must be true. Rhode returned his attention to Teegan, his neck red as a lobster. "Can we talk?"

What was there to say? He was an alcoholic. Her body shook and turned cold. She was going to have a panic attack at any moment.

"Hey," Sissy said, "you don't look well. Come outside on the back porch and sit down. I'll bring you some water." She whistled and her dogs came running, following them outside. Sissy guided Teegan by her elbow and eased her into the chair. "Lady, up."

Lady jumped into Teegan's lap.

"Just stroke her and take deep breaths. I'm going to grab that glass of water." She rushed from the deck and Teegan obeyed her instructions to breathe deeply as she petted the dog. Lady curled up in her lap and laid her head on Teegan's chest; her warmth radiated through Teegan's long-sleeved T-shirt. A smidge of tightness in her chest loosened, but this was shocking news that changed everything. He'd said he had a past and made mistakes, but this was different. This was…this was just like Mom.

Rhode stood cemented to the porch, licking his bottom lip, his fists clenched at his sides. Sissy returned with the water and knelt.

"Drink this. Little sips. Deep breaths in between."

Teegan sipped the water, the cool liquid satiating the burning fire in her throat.

"Better?"

"Some."

Sissy glanced up at her brother. "I'm going to leave you two alone." She squeezed his biceps and hurried inside.

"That's not how I wanted this to go down." Rhode tiptoed toward her.

Teegan gripped the glass tighter as memories surfaced. Mom forgetting them at school. Promising she'd stop. Getting sober and relapsing. No Christmas smells like here at the ranch: cinnamon, cloves and orange. No presents. No coming to games to see Misty cheer. All the fear, disappointment, anger and guilt resurfaced. She couldn't let her children go through those same agonies. This must be her punishment from God for her mistake. For picking up a hot guy at a bar after being drunk when she'd promised herself she never would touch a drop.

She might deserve this, but her twins did not.

"How exactly did you want it to go down? Why did you lie to me? You're a drunk *and* a liar?" The words shot out cold and sharp. Sharper than she'd intended, but fury bubbled to the surface. Not only at Rhode, but anger at herself and at her mother. The news had stoked the already simmering rage.

Rhode's lips pursed and his cheek pulsed. "I didn't lie. And I'm not a drunk. But I was. The day after our rendezvous, my brothers found me and I went straight to rehab. I haven't had a drop in over two years. Since that night. And you asked if I'd drank since then. I said no. That's not a lie."

"But you hid it from me! You know how I felt. I was up-front." She held Lady closer to her chest. "I can't let my children repeat my history. I won't."

"So now they're your children. The past couple of days, they've been ours." His own tone was sharp but not cold. It sizzled in red heat. "I wish I could go back and never have tasted a drop of liquor. But I did. I had no clue it was going to dig its claws into me and keep a hold until I lost everything. And I have. Lost everything. I regret it every single day." He pinched the bridge of his nose. "I planned to tell you, but it hasn't been the right time. I wanted you to know the real me so you could see I'm not who I once was, and I was afraid to tell you for fear you wouldn't let me see *our* babies."

"I'm not sure I'm going to." She placed the glass on the table next to the outdoor chair and stood, keeping Lady in her arms for support and warmth. Everything else about this moment was icy and empty. Could she take a chance and believe him? Her mom had held out for quite a long time, too, but in the end, she'd given in. How could she be sure Rhode wouldn't fall into the trap again? "Do you have cravings?"

He glanced away.

The cellar. The smell of the wine. "You didn't have claustrophobia, did you? You lied because the wine was enticing."

Rhode raked a hand through his hair, his longer bangs hanging in his eyes. "I didn't lie. The room was closing in on me, but, yes…it was because of the ache. The scent of the wine."

"Then you battle it still. You still want to drink."

Rhode's eyes shone. "Sometimes," he mumbled.

Teegan drew in a deep breath. Rhode was undeniably ashamed, but so had her mother been when she'd been sober. Maybe that's why she'd gone back to the bottle. Being numb was easier than carrying the pain of hurting loved ones. But that was a selfish move to play. "I think you're a decent person, Rhode. I do."

His eyes held hers, pleading. "I didn't drink any wine. I literally ran away."

"And can you honestly say you'll run every time?"

Rhode ran his tongue along his lower lip. "I hope so."

Hope wasn't enough for Teegan. "I need to be alone." She put Lady down and the dog trotted to the back door to be let inside. "I need to think."

She clambered off the back deck, putting space between them, and strode toward the barn. This was too much for her to even understand. She honestly blamed herself. If she hadn't made a terrible choice, she wouldn't be dealing with this. But then, she also wouldn't have the twins, and while the way they'd been conceived wasn't ideal, she didn't regret the babies. They were the most precious things in the world to her. A gift of God's mercy and grace, even in the jacked-up times. Teegan was thinking of the babies now.

Rhode wanted to be in their lives and might be great for a time. But what happened if he succumbed and spiraled? The babies would suffer. And they wouldn't understand why.

Teegan hadn't. When her mom was sober, she was amazing and, when she wasn't, she was neglectful and distant. Teegan always believed she hadn't met the standard of good enough for her mother. So she'd tried to be as good as she possibly could be in hopes Mom would come out of her room and love her. She'd kept the house spotless and the dishes done. Worked extra hard on her grades and joined academic clubs instead of sports. But the truth was it wouldn't matter how clean the house was or how great her grades had been.

Time passed, and she'd never measured up, which had led to crippling insecurity and the fight against becoming a people-pleaser. In college, a Christian psychology professor had spoken about insecurities and their consequences. Teegan had finally realized the problem hadn't been her, but her mother. Mom's disease had controlled her and no one but God had the power to help her fight it for good. Yet Teegan had spent all those years believing she could make her mother better. Make her love her.

But Rhode was a man of a faith—she didn't doubt that. And yet he couldn't even stay in a cellar without fearing he'd give in. He wasn't free; he was biding time. Teegan should extend him grace, but what if that grace opened the door for her children's pain? Teegan needed to shield them and protect them. What was she going to do?

She slunk onto a bale of hay outside the big red barn. Inside, horses pawed at stall doors and rustled the straw. The wind picked up and rattled the doors. How was she supposed to go back inside and pretend nothing happened? How was she going to bake cookies and watch movies and let her babies attach to this family—to their father—now knowing this enlightening information? The knowledge sent a ripple of confusion and disappointment through her. Teegan wasn't sure what she was hoping for. Nothing concerning them as a couple, but at least a committed and entirely involved dad.

She'd received a massive amount of money. An equally massive estate and a successful business in the blink of an eye and yet she felt more hollow and alone than she ever had before. No amount of money could fix this. Or the fact a killer was... She paused.

The hairs along her arms spiked as she immediately realized a presence. Teegan jumped to her feet as someone rushed her, knocking her to the cold, hard ground.

Her eyes widened under the moonlight

as the jester's mask came into full view. The white mask he wore contrasted with the dark hoodie.

"I'm going to get the last laugh," he said through a raspy voice as he brought up the large butcher knife, the blade glinting under the pale light.

She screamed and grabbed his forearm, trying to hold off the sharp blade, but he was strong. Unimaginably strong for her petite strength to match. A crack of gunfire erupted, giving the jester pause. Another shot fired and Rhode hollered her name.

The jester jumped to his feet and pointed the knife at her. "This isn't over." He hurled an insult and darted into the darkness.

Where he belonged.

Teegan sprang to her feet, her stomach in a tangle of knots and sweat slicking down her temples as she darted toward the sound of Rhode's voice. She ran straight into him and shrieked.

"It's okay. It's me. You're safe."

His brothers flew by them. "Which way?"

Bridge hollered, gripping his gun in his right hand.

"Behind the barn," Teegan said.

Bridge didn't slow and, like lightning, he vanished into the night.

Stone veered left, to hedge the other side.

Rhode cupped her face. "The babies are safe. Emily and Beau are inside to make sure everyone indoors is protected. Did he hurt you again?"

Teegan rubbed her head where it had smacked the solid earth as she'd fallen. Her hip smarted but, overall, she was in working order. "No. He came out of nowhere. How did he know we were here?"

Rhode released a long, heavy breath as he led her to the house. "He's watching, Teegan. He's watching."

Leading Teegan into the house, Rhode scanned the perimeter. All was quiet. Too quiet, and he sent up a silent prayer for his brothers' safety. This killer had a particular brand of weapon—a knife. But that didn't mean he wasn't also carrying a gun.

Seeing Teegan shake, he longed to hug her and protect her, but he didn't want to upset her further. She no longer trusted him—at least concerning their children—and Rhode understood.

She wasn't being ridiculous, over-the-top or excessively cautious. Teegan had endured the destructive consequences of alcoholism. While she hadn't revealed every detail of her childhood, she'd offered enough for him to feel the full impact it had seared into her soul.

Rhode wasn't naïve. Although he was now sober and relying on God, he had seen many men in rehab who had returned to the bottle when things grew difficult. Rhode kept his guard up on the daily, reminding himself he wasn't over it. The war still raged, and every day was a battle he had to trust God for. He completely understood Teegan's fear and hesitation.

He had no way of convincing her he wasn't like her mother. Because he knew how dark a path the drink had taken him on, the changes it had made, the man he'd become and hated but couldn't shake. Could he look her in the eye with utter confidence and tell her he would never succumb to temptation? No. He hoped. He prayed. But he wasn't arrogant enough to stake their children's lives on it. She'd been right. He couldn't even handle a wine cellar and wine had never been his drink of choice.

Rhode opened the kitchen door and Teegan went straight to the table. He grabbed a glass from the cabinet and flipped the water on, filling it to the brim, then he handed it to her. "Drink this."

Her hands trembled, and the water sloshed over the top of the glass, splashing onto the old farm table. "He said, 'This isn't over' and that he was going to get the last laugh. I think that's what he said before I passed out the last time too. What does that mean? The last laugh."

Rhode shook his head. "I don't know. Maybe, in his twisted mind, he believes you think receiving all of Lorna's fortune is some kind of joke or that you're laughing at the family. Maybe he thinks you've known all along you'd be receiving the inheritance—that you convinced Lorna through a long con to give up her money to you. It happens all the time, sadly."

"But Misty died before they read the will."

"We need to contact the attorneys and find out if any of the family members had recently inquired about the will. They could have persuaded the attorney to share the information."

Teegan sipped her water. "No one is above attempting a bribe in the Landoon family. If someone from the firm—not necessarily Lorna's personal attorneys—needed some money or wanted it, they might cough it up. I don't know how many attorneys are in the firm."

"We can find out." Rhode glanced up and Emily peered around the corner, her fiery red hair hanging around her shoulders, her brown eyes meeting his. He shook his head and she nodded. He noticed the gun in her hand. She'd steered Mama, Sissy and the babies into the living room. Beau must have gone out the front door. Rhode didn't see him and he couldn't hear his voice. Only the sounds of the Whos in Whoville singing "Welcome Christmas" and Sissy and Mama's voices accompanying the animated families.

But this wasn't the Grinch attempting to steal Christmas. This was a brutal killer bent on stealing the mother of his children. Rhode had to stop him. He would stop him.

"Are the children safe anywhere, Rhode? Am I?" Teegan pushed the glass away and covered her face with her hands. Her shoulders shook as she cried. But Rhode didn't offer physical comfort. He was unsure how to approach her now. Was he a friend or foe? Would she use all that new money to make sure he had no rights to his children? His past could easily be used against him. Her accusations of his sins would be right. She could take them to a judge and declare him guilty, stringing his past transgressions like a litany of his life.

Neglect of his family.

Neglect on the job.

Blundering a homicide investigation and allowing a killer to go free.

A one-night stand he couldn't even remember, and not just with Teegan. His past wasn't splotchy—it was stained and smeared red. Rhode didn't have a leg to stand on. He wouldn't be able to deny he'd missed the mark frequently.

He might lose his children before he ever began to truly know them.

And he could not blame Teegan for her actions. He might have done the same thing if he were in her place. For now, he had to focus on protecting her and catching this jester.

The back door opened and Stone entered first, a scowl along his brow. Bridge entered next and shook his head.

The jester had slipped them. Again.

"How you doing, Miss Albright?" Stone asked and rested his meaty palm on her shoulder.

She raised her head, tears streaking her dirty cheeks. "Not well, if I'm being honest. I'm working to be brave, but I'm not."

Rhode begged to differ. Teegan was the bravest woman he'd ever met. Resilient and determined. She had grit. She plainly didn't see it or believe it about herself.

"We'll keep working," Stone said.

Beau entered from the family room. "Nothing out front and no cars parked along the roads. He must have parked in field grass."

Mama entered the kitchen just then. Her jet-black hair—popped with a few silver strands—pulled back in a tight bun like her expression. "Teegan, sweetheart." She sat beside her, pulled her close then wrapped motherly arms around her.

Teegan crumpled against her and cried, letting it all out while Mama stroked her long blond hair.

"It's okay, baby girl. You just cry it out," Mama whispered and prayed over her. Rhode wanted to be the one to soothe her, but it was his fault she'd even been outside in the first place. And then it dawned: she'd probably never had a mother's comfort and his mama was nothing if not a nurturer.

Stone, Bridge and Beau slipped into the

family room, and Sissy clapped. "Yay. Christmas was saved. Say yay!"

The children clapped and hollered, "Yay!"

Rhode was intruding. He, too, exited the kitchen and entered the family room. The twins looked up and grinned, and Brook ran right for him. "Ho me."

He scooped her up, his heart growing like the Grinch's. His love for the babies burst from his chest. "Did you watch the Grinch?" He kissed her tiny brow and held her close. She didn't flinch or pull away. Rhode had Brook's trust. He wanted Teegan's too. He had no way to know how to garner it though.

"Why don't we watch *Frosty the Snowman* while we wait for Mama and Teegan?" Sissy said. Emily agreed and pressed the remote to stream the old cartoon. River busied himself banging the coaster on the already-nicked coffee table. He and his brothers had wrecked all of Mama's furniture growing up. Banging, clanging and jumping from anything solid as they'd played superheroes or cowboys.

Rhode settled in the overstuffed chair. Brook nestled on his lap. But his thoughts weren't on the snowman come to life. They were on the woman in the kitchen who needed a superhero.

And Rhode was the furthest thing from a superhero.

NINE

"Dude, this is awesome. Also, what's my cut of the treasure for diving and retrieving it?" Bridge asked. "I feel a big Christmas gift coming on."

Rhode glanced at Teegan as they stood by the Olympic-size swimming pool outside Lorna's home. In the past few years, the pool area had undergone an upgrade that replaced concrete with stone and added bright blue lounge chairs. The space now resembled a community center rather than a family gathering spot.

For the holiday, they'd strung white twinkling lights and changed the lounge cushions and towels to red and green since a heated pool meant swimming all year round.

Bridge sat with his back to the water,

scuba gear secured. He was ready to find the clue from the 1957 film *Make a Splash*. When Rhode had told him that the treasure was real, Bridge had turned back into that seventeen-year-old diving in Lorna's lake to discover riches untold. It had been almost three years since he'd seen Bridge's eyes light up like this. He'd been a shell of himself since the Christmas night Wendy, his former fiancée, had written him a note that she was leaving and not to come looking for her. He'd left the FBI around the same time and joined the family business with Stone.

None of the family had ever asked questions. If Bridge wanted them to know the details of his murky past, he would have told them. That's who Bridge was.

After last night's debacle, Teegan hadn't broken all ties. She wanted Rhode to handle the case. As far as their personal relationship, she wasn't rude, but the warmth growing between them had turned lukewarm. He hadn't brought up his role in the twins' lives. Teegan needed space and Rhode could give her that. He'd give her whatever she needed to make the right decision.

Rhode wanted to be a father.

"You get no cut of the treasure. This is something you do out the goodness of your heart," Rhode said.

Bridge adjusted his scuba mask. "That blows." He shoved the breathing apparatus into his mouth and entered the water as they watched him dive to the bottom of the ten-foot pool. The sun had set over an hour ago, and the employees had left the premises. Rhode didn't want curious eyes roaming and spilling the tea to the Landoon family that a treasure was real and they had been given clues. Teegan already had a massive target on her back. No need making it even larger.

Most of the day, he'd read files and kept in touch with Beau, who had been leading the case, and then he'd taken Teegan with him to shop for the twins. He'd purchased them a double-side car for outside and she said they'd love it—after he'd insisted he was buying them Christmas gifts no matter what. After, he'd helped her wrap presents—again at his insistence—and they'd had lunch at the ranch and he'd rocked the babies to sleep for their nap.

The water rippled and the lights of the pool cast shadows over Bridge, but he'd reached the drain. "I hope I'm right about this," Teegan said.

"I'm sure you are. It makes sense."

Awkward tension built, swirling like a winter breeze between them as they waited on Bridge.

Several minutes eked by.

"I think he has something." Teegan leaned over the pool, gawking below, and it appeared Bridge did have something. It evoked the image of the money tubes used by banks, but it was shorter, slenderer, and completely black like rubber.

Waterproof.

Bridge resurfaced and held it high, removing his breathing apparatus and grinning. "Victory!"

Rhode and Teegan laughed. Bridge swam to the side of the pool and handed Teegan the tube. "Figure you should do the honors. Can I stay and hear the next clue?"

Teegan chuckled. "Of course."

Bridge emerged from the water, took off his gear and eagerly waited next to Rhode.

Teegan opened the rubbery tube and inside a waterproof vial was a rolled-up slip of paper. She removed the clue, opened it, then read its contents. "'I can be myself when you're around. I can admit to the darkness that lurks in my mind and know you won't judge me for it. Oh, how I long to clear the cobwebs, step on the cockroaches of my stained past and tunnel my way to the light. Won't you help me find the light? I'm innocent.'"

Bridge scratched his head. "What in the world?"

Rhode stood, stumped. "Do you know what this quote is from? Which movie?"

Teegan's lips swerved to the left and she read it silently. "'I'm innocent.'" Her eyes looked out into nothing. Rhode wished Teegan would find him innocent, not judge his stained past. But that seemed impossible.

Teegan tapped her index finger against her chin. "She was in a film where she played an heiress accused of murdering her husband. I only remember that because she starred opposite Paul Newman. She has quite a lot of fond stories about him. He played a detective she fell in love with, but she murdered her husband and was manipulating the detective to believe in her innocence. I can't remember the title."

Rhode wasn't manipulating her to be in his children's lives. He swiped his phone from his back pocket and googled Lorna Landoon and Paul Newman. Several sites appeared. "*D is for Deception.*"

"Yes." Teegan snapped and pointed at him. "That's right. But where is she talking about?"

"A garage maybe?" Rhode shrugged. "Cockroaches. Cobwebs. Dark. Or a basement. Is there a basement, or could it be the wine cellar again?"

Teegan frowned. "No. Lorna would be

more creative. She wouldn't even drink the same blend of tea each afternoon. It wouldn't be the wine cellar."

"Tunneling to light sounds underground," Bridge offered with a boyish grin on his stubbly face.

"It does." Rhode scratched his temple then massaged it. He had a major headache threatening to burst through and his throat began the all-too-knowing dry ache. How many times had a small drink eased the thumping behind his eye or the tight muscles in his neck causing tension headaches? How many times had one little drink turned into an entire bottle or two and hours of blackness because he'd passed out?

More than he could count. He swallowed hard and reached into his pants' pocket, retrieving a stick of gum. Something to do, something to swallow.

Teegan eyed him and he caught the slight flash of judgment in her baby blues. But maybe it was his own paranoia.

"I'll keep thinking, and I might even find

blueprints to the house in Lorna's office. She designed this entire estate, including the labyrinth. She was a savvy woman." Her eyes filled with moisture, but Rhode kept his hands, which wanted to reach out for her, down at his sides, balled in fists.

Bridge checked his waterproof smartwatch and frowned. "She was definitely a cool lady. Look, I'd love to stick around, but Stone and I have to go to a recovery site. He just texted the scene is clear. Sissy's already there with the mother."

The young boy had died of suicide after being bullied online. His mother had heard the gunfire but was too late to intervene. Rhode inwardly cringed at the tragedy. He needed to stay on this case and keep the mother of his children protected.

"We'll keep you posted," Rhode said as Bridge carried his gear to his car.

"Should we search?" Rhode asked just as his phone rang. "It's Beau." He answered. "Hey, is this about Teegan's case? If so, I'm going to put us on speaker."

"Cool. It is," Beau said.

Rhode pressed the speaker button. "Okay, go."

"I told you about that boyfriend of Misty's that was trouble. Well, it's not him."

"How do you know?" Rhode asked.

"Because the Cedar Springs police found him an hour ago in the woods behind Lorna's estate. He's dead."

"Dead?" Teegan said and pressed her hand against her mouth. "Kenny Lee? Isn't that the name of the guy?"

"Yes," Beau said. "He was stabbed in the woods and left there, likely on the same day your sister was killed."

"So it wasn't a murder-suicide. Not if he has multiple stab wounds, right?"

"He didn't. It was one cut to the carotid. He followed her, killed her, and then went into the woods and slit his own throat. It's been done before in this manner. Dom said he'll know more once the autopsy is completed, but he's not ruling that out."

Teegan shuddered. "But it's not him.

Someone is still coming after me and with a big fat knife."

A heavy sigh filtered through the line. "Yeah, I have a theory about that. Let's say Kenny Lee followed Misty to Texas. He killed her. Then he ran. You said you saw Charlie Landoon pass you. What if Charlie was in the house and witnessed Kenny kill her? He could have followed Kenny into the woods, stolen the knife, killed him and is using it now. For all he knows, no one will ever find Kenny's body. With Kenny's prints on the knife, it would lead to him."

But they had found the body, so the potential jig was up.

"They're keeping it out of the news, but the media will only allow it so long," Beau added. "If Charlie—or someone else in the family—is doing it, they don't know Kenny has been found. Yet."

Rhode rubbed his temples again. "Did they find bluebonnets near him? And why would Kenny or Charlie kill Addie James?"

"Maybe it wasn't Charlie. Maybe some other Landoon, like Peter, had been at the house. Charlie is the only car and person you saw, Teegan. But that doesn't mean he was the only one there."

Teegan's mind spun. There were numerous variables. The suspects endless. The motive unclear. "Have the police talked to Peter?"

Beau cleared his throat. "Apparently, Peter is out of the country on business."

"Then he can't be the person after me."

Rhode's expression seemed a cross between apology and disbelief, looking at her like Rachel looked at Joey on *Friends* when he said something stupid. Next, he'd be telling her, "You're so pretty." Rhode sighed. "Just because someone says he's out of the country and, even if we can find a plane ticket or manifest with his name on it, it doesn't mean he's actually out of the country. People lie and fake their whereabouts all the time, especially if they're using private or chartered planes."

True. And Peter absolutely had the funds to bribe private charters. A Landoon flying commercial would be like someone not covering their heart during the National Anthem or a preacher taking the Lord's name in vain. "Well then, what do we do?"

"What we always do," Rhode said. "Ferret out the truth and watch our backs."

"When I know more," Beau said, "you will too." He ended the call, and Rhode shoved his phone into the back pocket of the worn jeans he'd been wearing with a pair of old cowboy boots and a long-sleeved Henley that was as black as his hair and eyes.

Teegan couldn't let physical attraction dictate her life. Misty had done that and it ended in a Kenny Lee. Not that Rhode was a Kenny Lee. He'd never hit a woman, but then, if he wasn't sober, she didn't know what he would be capable of doing.

Teegan checked her phone. No texts from Sissy or Emily, but she didn't want the babies to be an imposition. Rhode's mother, Marisol, had been overwhelmingly and unexpectedly kind. When she'd pulled her into an embrace after Teegan's attack on the ranch, she'd felt safe and loved in a nurturing way she never had before. Mom's affection had appeared during short bursts of sobriety. Being loved by Marisol had been exactly what she'd needed.

"I should pick up the children. I don't want them to overstay their welcome and it's going to be their bedtime soon."

"Teegan, those babies have been the best thing in our family in a long time. They are not, nor will they ever be, an imposition on our big ole family. They fit right in."

A big family. A loving, supportive family. The Spencers loved each other, despite their shortcoming and failures. Could Teegan also extend that grace to Rhode as his own family had? They were adults, and if he ended up in the gutter again, they would be able to handle the disappointment. Children didn't understand. They blamed themselves.

"Let's see if we can't figure out where the next clue is. Maybe we should watch *D is for Deception*. The backdrop during this scene might give us an idea of where to look in the house or on the property. I'll call and tell them we'll pick the twins up later."

Teegan reluctantly agreed. The movie and treasure hunting might take her mind off the chaos going on in her real life. She headed for the theater room and found the film, then got it ready.

Her phone rang, and she saw it was the attorney's office. Her stomach bottomed out. "Hello?"

"Hi, Miss Albright. It's Scott Carmichael. I'm sorry to call after five. But business hours are laughable in this line of work."

"No worries. Is everything alright?"

Scott sighed. "Yes, but because we handled Lorna's estate and you haven't fired us, we're your attorneys now and you should know that the Landoon family has officially contested the will and hired big guns. Bernstein, Wilcox and Bailey."

"What does that mean exactly?" Was Teegan out of a home again? Would the money be frozen? Not that she'd used any of it yet.

"You can only contest a Last Will and

Testament during the probate process if there's a valid legal question about the document or process under which it was created. They're stating she didn't have testamentary capacity."

"Mental capacity?" Teegan asked.

"Yes. It's a common legal reason to contest a will," Scott said. "But they're also stating 'Under the influence,' which means someone had unduly influenced her at the time of signing. A common example would be a full-time caregiver who has taken complete control of all an elderly parent's assets, decisions and day-to-day life, and has been fully in charge of him or her, influencing them to agree to just about anything, including signing a will that might not be what they want."

"But I didn't!" Teegan's heart slammed into overdrive. "I never discussed this with her. I assumed when she passed, I'd be looking for a new job. And she was sharp as a tack, Scott. Surely, you know this or Sylvia, who often handled Lorna's affairs at the firm."

"We know this, Miss Albright."

"Call me Teegan." They were around the same age and if things were about to get sticky—which they were—they might as well be on a first-name basis with one another.

"Teegan, then. I didn't call to upset you but to inform you. I don't see the court throwing it out. It will look at all the facts in the case and decide based on what is provable. Wills are, generally, upheld, and sibling disagreements after a parent's death usually subside with time."

"So I have nothing to worry about?"

"No. But you need to understand that the assets will be frozen until court."

"Can I live in the house still or do I need to find a new place? I have babies and no job." Panic fluttered in her chest.

"You have until December twenty-fourth by 8:00 a.m. to be out. The family thinks that's generous."

That was two days away. She had to find a new place by Christmas Eve morning? Where would her babies celebrate? Rhode would offer the ranch and she would have to accept, without a doubt, but that felt wrong since she'd all but told him his relationship with the babies was in limbo. She wasn't a user like that.

"Lorna's money is frozen, so you cannot spend it or have control over the thoroughbred business, but the good news is, neither can the Landoon family."

"I understand. Thank you."

"If you need anything, call the office."

Teegan hung up and laid her head on the counter in the projector booth. Two days.

When Rhode entered the room, she raised her head. He was grinning.

"The kids are having a ball and so is the family. They've offered to keep them overnight. And if Stone is offering, he means it. He's not what I'd call a pushover."

Teegan didn't think so either. "If they're sure, then that's alright by me. They sleep well anywhere, so I'm not worried about that, but tell them if they get fussy and ask for me, I'll come and pick them up."

Rhode ran his thumbs along his phone's

keyboard then pocketed the device. "Done. What's going on?"

"One of Lorna's attorneys called." She relayed the message to Rhode. "I'm not worried about the money. But to leave on Christmas Eve? I'd had such plans for River and Brook. I overindulged in gifts and wanted them to have a stable Christmas, and we're like a ship out at sea during a tropical storm. Tossed here and there and… it's all the things I don't want for them." She laid her head on the table again and tried not to bawl and squall. This was embarrassing and overwhelming, and she'd all but told Rhode he couldn't be a father. If he couldn't be a dad, then he couldn't be her comfort or confidante either. That wasn't fair to him or to her.

"You had no way of knowing you'd inherit this money or that there would be a freeze on the accounts."

Which meant they'd have to cancel the security company coming. She had no means to pay them.

"Sometimes things beyond our control

happen and we have to make do. You know the whole lemons and lemonade spiel."

"I have all the lemons and no sugar for the drink."

"Now's probably not a good time to say, 'I'll give you some sugar.'" He softly snorted, and she actually found she could laugh.

He'd given her some sugar once before and that had led to more sugar than they should have partaken and resulted in twins. "Let's just watch this movie—I googled where the line fits. It's about three-quarters through and I've set it to start there."

Lorna was in a large dining room, her hair swept up and her lips a perfect shade of crimson.

Paul Newman rushed into the room, his chest heaving. "Darla," he whispered. "They found the gun. Your prints are on it. Have you lied to me all this time? How can I have fallen in love with...a murderer?"

Lorna's eyes pooled as she drank a deep finger of whiskey. "How can you even ask me that? You know me. I can be myself when you're around. I can admit to the darkness that lurks in my mind and know you won't judge me for it. But you're judging me now. How can we have a future without mutual trust?"

"There is no future when they match the gun with the bullet that killed your husband. I know you haven't been squeaky clean but..."

"Oh, how I long to clear the cobwebs, step on the cockroaches of my stained past and tunnel my way to the light. Oh, won't you help me?" She kissed Paul Newman, leaving red lipstick on his mouth. "I'm innocent. I know how it looks." She gripped his suit lapels. "But you must believe me. I don't care what anyone else thinks of me. Only you, Thomas."

Paul pushed her away and turned his back. Lorna dramatically cried out and rushed from the room, tripping over the dining room rug. Paul's character—Thomas—dropped to his knees and held her. "I believe you. I do."

Then he showed her with a passionate kiss that had Teegan wondering if it was

acting or if there might be something behind it for real. Lorna had only been married a brief time to a famous director, but
shortly after the twins were born, he filed
for divorce. She and a nanny raised the children, but Lorna had many suitors before
and after her marriage.

That's when she noticed the rug.

"Rhode. That rug. It's in the dining room.
Of this house."

Rhode followed Teegan into the room
that overlooked the front of the estate. A
massive dining room table was the focal
point. The gold Christmas runner on the
tabletop and pots of real poinsettias created
a festive atmosphere. The large Oriental
rug underneath the table was in shades of
navy, blue and burgundy.

Glancing at the large foyer, he snapped
his fingers. "Let's move the table into the
foyer so we can roll back the rug."

Teegan nodded and went to work moving
the twenty dining chairs to the sides of the
dining room and then, together, they lifted

the table and pivoted toward the foyer. Once the table was removed from the rug, they worked to roll it up under the windows.

"I don't see anything." Teegan huffed and planted her hands on her hips.

"Were you expecting some kind of hatch or trap door handle?" Dropping to his knees, he used his cell phone's flashlight to study the hardwood.

"I was hoping for one. Leave it to Lorna to not be easy." She mimicked Rhode and began searching the floor with her hands.

If there was a secret passage that led to a tunnel under the house, this was where it had to be. Rhode and Teegan pressed and pulled on every piece of flooring, but nothing turned up.

"What are we missing?" Rhode sat on his heels and scoured the room, searching for any kind of clue. Had Lorna Landoon been mentally unstable? Had she started to bury a treasure and then petered out? Did they have the clue wrong?

Teegan tiptoed along the uncovered floor,

slightly pressing with her feet for give, a frown lining her brow.

Rhode stood, his right knee cracking. "Maybe the rug is the clue to the right location but we have the method wrong." His hands glided along the cream-colored walls and he paid close attention to the chair railing. Moving a large hutch with china, he felt along the back of the wall and continued around the room until he reached two sconces flanked by a painting almost as tall as himself.

"Hey, weren't these in the movie too?" he asked.

Teegan glanced up, frustration still twisting her face. She eyed the sconces and tilted her head to the side. "Yeah. Good eye."

He chalked it up to his mom dragging him and Sissy along as children to estate sales. Mama loved antiques. After a moment, he pulled on the right sconce and it gave way. A creaking and groaning filled the air as the painting cracked open.

"It's like something out of that movie *Clue*. Did you see it?"

"I did. Loved that game as a kid. I beat Bridge and Stone every time, but Sissy knew my tells and she was harder to fool."

"It's a secret passage from the conservatory to the kitchen!" Teegan mimicked Miss Scarlet. Rhode wasn't sure that was the exact line, but he smiled anyway.

Rhode put some muscle into it and opened the painting—a front for a heavy wooden door. Cobwebs shivered at the draft, and he held up his cell phone light. "Stairs."

Concrete.

"Well? What are we waiting for?"

"Nothing, I guess. Let's do this." Rhode drew his weapon and glanced at Teegan. "Just in case."

"In case of critters or killers?"

"Both. I don't like either one."

"Same." Teegan inched up behind him as if he were an invincible shield and he couldn't deny he liked the way she trusted in him, confident he could and would protect her. If only she'd trust him in other areas.

Rhode started down and Teegan followed.

Her hand rested on his left shoulder, her cell flashlight shining from her other hand as they descended the cement stairs. The walls were cool and concrete, covered in cobwebs and a few spiders. Chill bumps raised on his arms. It definitely felt like winter down here.

A squeak sent Teegan's grasp tighter on Rhode's shoulder. "What was that?"

"What do you think it was?"

"A mouse or a rat."

"You'd be right."

Teegan shuddered and scooted closer to him, her sweet scent teasing his senses. "Why do you think she had this built?"

"Good question. Could be because she had the funds and simply wanted to. Could be to hide things like treasure. The question is, does the family know it's here?"

"No one has mentioned it, but surely one of them does. Why would Lorna not tell anyone, including the family? Plus, the blueprints are in the office."

"Why didn't we just look at that then? Didn't you say you planned to?"

Teegan chuckled. "I don't know. I guess the hunt feels so Indiana Jones-like. All we're missing is the hat and the whip."

"And the cool leather jacket," Rhode added.

"Well, there's that. You'd look good dressed like Indy."

Rhode's gut tightened and the air grew thick.

Teegan cleared her throat. "I just mean that you're adventurous."

Rhode was pretty sure she was covering for blurting out a compliment at best, flirtation at worst, because she'd all but told him he couldn't be in their lives personally. She was like a bad case of whiplash.

The old concrete steps spiraled then ended, leaving a long dark corridor that stretched forward. "Doesn't look like any light at the end of the tunnel," he said.

"Do we keep going or turn back?"

He shined the light along the walls and the floor. "We came for a clue—or the treasure. Let's find it."

Using their cell phone lights, Rhode felt along the wall.

A scraping along the cement caught his attention. "Did you hear that?"

They paused, listening.

"No," Teegan whispered and scooched closer to Rhode. "What was it?"

"I'm not sure." He put his index finger to his lips. "Turn off your light."

"Are you insane?" She drew out the *s*.

He held her forearm. "I won't let go of your arm. Just turn it off." He switched off his cell phone light and she finally extinguished hers.

Tangible darkness engulfed them and she shivered against him. Holding her wrist, he felt her quickening heartrate thump against his fingers. Skittering along the walls brought ice to Rhode's spine but he focused on the scraping noise—like boots scuffing cement.

Their breathing overrode the rodents and bugs, and the shuffling silenced. Rhode must be hearing things. No one knew about this tunnel. And even if they did, no one could possibly know that he and Teegan were planning to come down here.

Unless they were being watched or the killer had camped out in this place. And if that was the case, they'd willingly walked into the lion's den.

"I don't hear anything, Rhode, and I'm starting to freak out. This was a bad idea."

She might not be wrong.

"Just give it a few more seconds. Please," he murmured.

The noise had come from the way they'd entered. Their only choice was to keep moving forward and hope there was light at the end of the tunnel—literal light. Otherwise, things were going to get dicey.

Thunk. Thunk.

Teegan gripped his biceps. "I heard that. I heard it that time, Rhode. We're not alone down here."

"No. No, we're not."

TEN

"I want you to keep going forward. I'm going to stay right here and when he catches up to us, I'll be waiting," Rhode whispered.

Teegan's stomach jittered. "No. I can't leave you. What if he kills you?"

"What if you stay and he kills us both? Do we want our children to grow up without any parents?"

Rhode made a valid point. But she didn't want him to risk his life. She might be unsure of how much time he could be with the children given his past, and the fact he admitted to wanting to drink, but she definitely didn't want him dead.

"Why don't we both leave? Just hurry to the end and find a safe place? You don't have to be a hero."

"I'm not trying to be a hero, Teegan. I'm

just trying to keep the mother of my children alive. Go. I don't know how much time we have. Whoever is down here clearly knows about the tunnel and that means he might have better knowledge of where it leads. He's at an advantage."

Teegan could argue, and they'd both catch their deaths, or she could trust Rhode. He'd been a detective and a good one—she knew it deep down. He was capable and trustworthy—at least when he was sober.

"Okay." Teegan turned and prayed God would keep them safe. The tunnel narrowed and something crunched under her shoes. Probably a cockroach or some other creepy-crawly she despised. Bugs gave her the heebie-jeebies. Why on earth would Lorna build a tunnel under her estate? It's not like tornadoes were prevalent in the hill country.

As she felt along the wall, she noticed a dip. It wasn't sharp or jagged, just a little uneven. She paused, listened. Nothing. No footsteps. Not a single peep. It raised the hairs on her neck and arms.

What if the jester had hurt Rhode? Killed him? Wouldn't she have heard something?

She should keep going but the dip in the wall… She ran her hands until she felt an opening. But to know for sure if a clue was inside, she'd have to go in blindly. Curling her nose and glancing behind her, she fought the anxiety rising in her belly.

She should keep going, but they might not have another chance. And what if the person down here was searching for the clue too? Teegan had to pause. Had to find it first.

She groaned, pulled her sweatshirt sleeve over her hand like a glove and then reached inside. She couldn't feel anything with the heavy material over her fingers. Just great.

Inhaling a deep breath, she released the fabric and sticky cobwebs entangled her exposed flesh.

With cobwebs came spiders and other icky creatures. Pushing past fear, she maneuvered her hand, thrusting it deep into the tight space, and her fingers brushed against something rubbery and long, like a tube.

She grasped it and yanked it out. The clue. She had another clue.

Teegan could open it later. For now, she had to do as Rhode had instructed and haul it out of this tunnel. She wasn't sure how long she'd been digging around in the wall. Couldn't have been more than seconds. Clutching the tube, she darted one last glance toward Rhode, who was engulfed in darkness with a psychotic person who got his thrills and chills wearing a jester mask and carrying a butcher knife. Did no one tell him that was Horror Movie 101, making it cliché?

Of course, she had all the bravado she needed at the moment. She wasn't the one in the tunnel confronting the killer. She was the one running away.

Darting down the corridor, she kept her hand along the wall to help guide her and hoped nothing lay in front of her to trip on. She silently prayed for Rhode as gunfire echoed in the tunnel, deafening her. She shrieked and cried out, "Rhode!"

Did she go back? Keep running ahead? Rhode would be furious if she returned for him, but she couldn't leave him alone in the tunnel with a killer. Unless…had Rhode shot him?

A scuffle sounded. Two men.

Neither dead—yet.

She switched on her cell phone flashlight and used it to search for anything that might serve as a weapon. Lying in the corner was a piece of rock that had fallen from the wall. Teegan wasted no time, retrieved it, then switched off the light and kept to the side of the tunnel wall as she headed in the direction of the fight ensuing up ahead.

Rhode's phone must have fallen in the commotion. A faint glow from the tunnel floor peeked through the darkness and illuminated a narrow path for Teegan to follow.

Rhode punched the jester in the face, and he dropped, but then he grabbed Rhode by the legs and brought him down with a hard thud.

Straddling Rhode, the jester raised his arm. And Teegan went in for the strike. She slammed the rock into the back of the jester's head and he collapsed to the floor but then regained his footing and came for Teegan.

His presence moved into her space like a whirling tornado and slammed her against the cement wall, her head banging against rock. Little white pinpricks of light dotted her eyes and she fought to keep from blacking out. Hands wrapped around her throat but then suddenly he was ripped away from her.

Rhode!

Unable to see, she could only listen to the grunts of two men battling it out to the death. She could not, would not, stand there doing nothing. She switched on the flashlight again, found the rock and looked up to see the man in the hoodie straddling Rhode. Teegan rushed him, using the rock and slamming it into the back of his head again.

He fell to his side, unmoving this time.

"Rhode. Are you okay?"

Rhode grunted and stood over the attacker, who was lying on his stomach, listless. Panic replaced relief. "Oh no. Rhode! Did I kill him?" She hadn't meant to kill him, even if she had been defending Rhode.

Rhode rolled the man over using his foot.

But he wasn't wearing a mask or wielding a knife.

Teegan used her flashlight and stared at Dexter Landoon's bloody face.

Dexter Landoon was the jester? He'd killed his own mother and Misty? Possibly Addie too? Why?

"I'm so confused right now."

Rhode released a heavy breath and checked Dexter's pulse. "Join the club." He peered up at her. "He's alive."

"Good. Now he can go to prison where he belongs."

"Speaking of being where one belongs, what happened to following directions? You should be out of the tunnel and to safety by now. *Where. You. Belong.*" His voice was raspy and clipped, and the scowl on his face revealed just how thoroughly upset he was.

"First of all, you're not the boss of me. Second, I heard a gunshot and fighting. I couldn't tuck tail and leave you here alone. And before you go all 'I'm a dude and can take care of myself,' don't. You needed help and I helped you."

Rhode gawked at her, blood trickling from his bottom lip. He undid his belt and used it to secure Dexter Landoon's hands behind his back. "We'll discuss this more in depth after we question him and once my lip stops bleeding. Are you alright?" He finished securing the knocked-out-cold Dexter and stood, running his cell light over her face. He paused at her neck and his eyes flashed with dark fury. Running his index finger along her throat, he frowned. "He hurt you," he murmured.

He had. But right now, she was feeling far from hurt. A flurry of flutters filled her belly at his touch along her skin. Not so much his actual touch but the way his eyes went from fury to something that unsettled her and drew her. His thumb grazed her jawbone, his eyes on hers, and his Adam's apple bobbed hard when he swallowed.

"I'm fine," she squeaked through a dry mouth.

Rhode inched into her personal space. "Are you sure?" he whispered.

She couldn't deny she was woozy, but it had nothing to do with Dexter choking her or slamming her against the wall. The air thickened, sweet and warm. Rhode's minty breath with a hint of cinnamon brought back a rush of memory.

He's a coward. And a fool for walking away from you. You're smart, funny...and beautiful.

"You think I'm beautiful," she blurted breathlessly.

"I do."

"And smart."

"Absolutely—minus the stunt you just pulled."

She grinned. "And funny."

Rhode squinted and framed her face. "Yes." His dark eyes held her captive and every brain cell withered and died at his expression. Not a man eyeing a woman he wanted to hook up with. This was something deeper. Stronger. Pure. It terrified and enthralled her all at once and her heartrate spiked until it throbbed in her ears.

A long, dark lock of hair hung in his eyes and she slowly slid it behind his ear. "I had to save you."

His nose grazed hers, his lips a hairbreadth from hers. "Then I owe you a thank you," he murmured, his lips touching hers as he pronounced each word.

Teegan's eyes automatically closed as she fell headlong into the moment. "I suppose you do."

Sliding his hand from her cheek into her hair, his lips pressed against hers. Soft but urgent. Warm and full.

"Hey! Let me go!"

Dexter had woken.

Rhode broke the kiss that hadn't really gotten off the ground yet, but she was certainly floating.

And floating had never landed her anywhere solid. She'd fallen into a whirlwind romance with her former fiancé, Darryl. He'd left her before the wedding.

It was time to find sure footing.

Rhode Spencer wasn't it.

Even if she wanted to trust him. Even if he'd proven trustworthy. He had an anchor tied around his neck and it was only a matter of time before it dragged them both under.

Rhode towered over Dexter Landoon. He'd hauled the jerk up and had him sit against the tunnel wall. He had every intention of calling Dom, but he wanted to question Dexter first. A PI had a different set of rules and the word "lawyer" meant nothing to him.

He glanced back at Teegan, who stood with her arms crossed at her chest and a thumbnail in between her teeth. Had they almost kissed five minutes ago? He'd been terrified to see her still in the tunnel and then furious, but her loyalty, concern and bravery had filled his heart with admiration and mad respect. Teegan was a fighter. A survivor and an all-around awesome woman. She was also stubborn, rebellious and defiant. And he kinda admired that too.

No denying she revved his pulse like a V10 engine.

He hadn't been able to resist her. But he was impulsive and his restraint was pretty much nil, which is why he'd ended up down the path he'd been on over two years ago. Teegan could not become his new addiction, but he'd wanted to taste her more than a drop of liquor. Wanted to find comfort in her embrace and share a tender moment to show… What? Words formed in his mind but they were words he couldn't attach to. Word that were not "thank you." One didn't thank a person with a kiss—not like that. The atmosphere had been crackling like a raging wildfire in a drought.

It had been a good thing for Dexter Landoon to wake.

"Why am I bound? I'm calling the police."

"You were trespassing, for one," Rhode

said, now focused on the problem at hand. "Assets are frozen, but Miss Albright has until Christmas Eve to vacate. And lurking in a dark tunnel at night is suspicious to say the least. Why are you here? How did you know about the tunnel or that we were down here?"

Dexter leaned his head against the concrete wall. "Miss Albright assaulted me. I'll be bringing charges against you both. I have the gash on my head to prove it."

"You have no gash, I checked. And we were acting in self-defense. Why are you trying to kill Miss Albright?" Rhode shined the cell flashlight in Dexter's direction but not into his face. He'd only received a squint and Rhode wanted to see his natural facial reactions.

Dexter's eyes grew wide. "I didn't kill— or attempt to kill—anyone. Everyone in my family knows about this tunnel and the other secret passages that lead here and to the stables."

"There are multiple passages?"

"Yes. They all lead to this one connecting tunnel."

That explained how an intruder showed up in Teegan's room and how he disappeared so many times with no trace. He was using the secret passages to this tunnel.

"In my mother's earlier days, she didn't want the staff seen. You know, like at Disney World. They use underground tunnels to travel from place to place. She still had some of her snobbery in her. Staff should be working without being seen. Eventually that changed and she stopped using them. But our children would occasionally still play down here. How do you know about the tunnel?"

"Doesn't matter." And he was the one asking questions. He'd patted him down. No weapon. No butcher knife. "You're not dressed in a fancy suit. You're in the same kind of clothing the jester wore when he tried to kill Miss Albright. When he murdered her sister and your mother. Explain."

Dexter heaved a sigh. "I don't have to explain anything, but I will. I'm dressed in black because I didn't want to be seen. I am in the tunnel because I wanted something from the house before Evangeline takes the place, so I thought I'd sneak in and grab it and go. I had no idea the two of you would be down here. It scared me. Why are you here?"

"Doesn't matter. What is it you wanted?"

Dexter's face turned smug. "Doesn't matter."

Fair enough.

"If you need something you don't want your sister to know about, we might be able to help you retrieve it. If your story checks out, and right now I'm not so sure." Dexter might be the killer. Or he was here to kill Teegan to protect his grandson, Peter, who had ties to Addie and Teegan and free access to the house. He could have killed Kenny Lee, Misty's ex too.

"Evangeline is a money mosquito. She'll suck the estate dry. And while I'm not salivating like wolves over fat lambs, I do want a few things. One of which is a deed to a property my mom owned in Austin. It belonged to her daddy and is worth a fortune. Evangeline doesn't know about it."

"Why not?"

"My mother never told her, but I knew. I've seen the files. Upstairs. The maps and the deed as well as any other documents. I wanted them before Evangeline takes possession. That property is worth far more than all of Mother's assets combined. Oil property."

Dexter was going to sneak and steal it. No wonder he hadn't seemed interested over the reading of the Will and Last Testament. All he'd wanted was the old Landoon real estate.

"I thought Mother would will it to me. I was surprised that she didn't. If you give me that, I'll help you fight Evangeline and Glen. I'll back up that Mother wasn't out of her mind or under mental duress at the time."

Teegan looked at Rhode for guidance.

"That will be something Teegan needs to think about for more than two seconds, and you haven't been cleared as the jester.

Just because you don't have the mask and knife doesn't mean you didn't do it."

Dexter snorted. "Fine. Do whatever tests you need. You want DNA? Swab me. Need fingerprints? Have at it. I did not kill anyone. I shouldn't have been skulking around like a two-bit criminal, I agree. But I feared if I mentioned it to Teegan, it might end up being discussed and Evangeline would get wind of it."

Rhode wasn't so sure he believed Dexter. Often, criminals who thought they couldn't be caught were willing to give DNA samples as well as take polygraphs. Cold and calculated sociopaths often passed them. And there might not be any DNA on either victim. His prints would be in the house and should be. He was Lorna's son.

"I'll consider it," Teegan said. "I never asked for or expected to receive all of Lorna's things. I was as shocked as anyone else."

Dexter shifted and readjusted his bound hands. "I believe you. My mother was mischievous and a drama queen until the end. We loved it as children. As adults, we weren't as amused by it. Evangeline believes this was Mother's last little fun with the family."

Like a last laugh. Exactly what the killer had said to Teegan.

"Cutting you out of a will? That's going beyond hidden property, tunnels and rumors of treasure," Teegan said.

"I didn't say *I* believed that. I think Mother was sick of Evangeline, Glen and Charlie's mooching and money-grubbing hands. I don't understand why she cut myself and Peter out. We've been good with our inheritance. We didn't squander it and we work. We've invested and doubled our money. But I suppose she had her reasons." He closed his eyes. "My head hurts."

He was all too calm about this. And he had been skulking around. Rhode wasn't sure he was lying, but he was certain Dexter wasn't telling the whole tale. Rhode wanted to see those property maps himself. If it was worth more than Lorna's estate and the money she'd left, including the thoroughbred business—that would be over a billion dollars easy. The Landoons could split that and still have money to last long after they passed on. Unless they squandered it, but Rhode couldn't imagine going broke in this lifetime with that amount of money. They'd have to buy yachts and trips and a slew of property to run through that kind of wealth.

They were willing to kick a single mom of twins onto the street at Christmas, so it was possible they were just fat enough at heart to glutton themselves on the finances with anything and everything they laid their eyes on.

"If you're cleared by the police, we'll discuss it. I won't say anything to Evangeline and…and I'll find the files and take them with me. For now." Teegan's shoulders had pulled back and she'd raised her chin. It was more than he'd do for a man who might have murdered his own mother and two other women. But it was Teegan's money now. If it was truly oil property, then Teegan and the babies were set for many lifetimes. Generations to come would never worry about finances again.

Rhode wasn't sure how to feel about that. He barely had two pennies to rub together. What could he possibly provide except anxiety to Teegan, who would constantly fear a relapse? It wasn't like he didn't have that same fear. Even in this moment, his nerves purred at the thought of amber liquid burning its way down his gullet to his belly, creating a heated and soothing warmth. Languid.

She'd have nine ducks and a cow if he revealed that temptation, that urge. Instead, he pushed it out with a reminder that God's grace was sufficient for him. In this moment. This lie that swirled around his mind telling him that one drink wasn't going to kill him. It would ease his anxiety and fear.

Lies. God was his peace. God was his calm in the storm. And the thirst was like a tempest he'd never experienced before.

Tossing him like a rag doll. Coaxing him to jump overboard into still waters.

But Jesus led him beside real still waters. Waters of the Word that would renew his mind. Keep him focused on things above.

"Did you hear me, Rhode?" Teegan asked and cocked her head, studying him. She had his number. Recognized the signs of craving. How could she not?

Rhode hadn't heard her. He'd been in a battle.

"I said, we need to get out of the tunnel and call the police now. Let Dom figure it out."

"Right. Yes. Sorry." He shook his rattled head, hoping the thoughts would shake out and bring him back to a level head. Back to the moment. He cleared his parched throat and hauled up Dexter. They walked back the way they'd begun and returned to the dining room. He closed the painting behind him.

Rhode sat him in a chair, leaving the belt on his wrists. He called Dom and woke up him up, giving him the rundown. "He'll be here in twenty minutes, but he asked if he should just temporarily move in."

"Can I talk to you?" Teegan asked. "In private?"

Was she going to call out his earlier war with the bottle? Nerves knotted his gut, but he followed her a few feet away, out of earshot but where Rhode could keep an eye on Dexter. "What's up?"

"I found it," she whispered. "The clue. It was inside a divot in the wall. Like in the *Temple of Doom*."

"Bugs?"

She wrinkled her nose and nodded. "But I have it. I still need to read it. Thought I'll wait until he's gone."

"Good call and good work."

"Are you okay?" she asked. "You went away for a few minutes and…and I know that forlorn expression. I saw it on my mom when she was sober but wishing she wasn't."

"I'm fine."

"She said that too." Her mouth turned hard.

"Teegan, I'm not sharing that part of my

life with you. You've made it clear it's keeping me from being in my kids' lives. And while I get it—I understand your thinking and fear—know I'm thinking the same thing. I'm fearing the same thing. But more than fearing I'll drink again, I fear I won't get to know my children. I won't be a good dad. I have nothing to offer them. And you threatening me with withholding them from me, it kinda makes me not want to share my struggles with you." He folded his arms over his chest, waiting on her reply.

Her cheeks tinged pink and she kicked her toe along the floor. "I'm sorry. I don't mean to be without mercy or compassion, Rhode. Truly. But...you can't begin to know what I went through my whole life until Mom died. You can't understand how much I want my children to have a normal life. A stable life. I don't want to live in fear. You think I like the burning and gnawing sensation in my stomach? I don't." She closed her eyes. "But the children come first. Always and in every way."

"But you let me kiss you. I can't be in our

children's lives, but I can do that? If that's not personal, I don't know what is."

She flinched at his harsh tone, the truth in his words.

"That was a mistake. It won't happen again. There is no you and me. Not even if I allow you in the children's lives. I can at least control that narrative. But I can't trust you. Not with my heart. And I don't want our babies to lose theirs to you either. Because you'll break them. I know it. And, deep down, I think you know it too." While her tone was low and her words soft, they hit with a one-two punch. A total knock-out. Below the belt.

He'd heard the same words from his family when he'd come out of rehab. *Trust has to be earned back. One day at a time.* And he had—earned their trust. They hadn't held his past, his sins, against him. Neither had God. But, at the moment, it felt like God was punishing him in the worst way for his mess-ups. Punishing him by revealing he had children then stealing them away.

Maybe Teegan was right.

Maybe he was a grade-A loser who had no business in their lives. He had nothing to give but the possibility of screwing them up mentally and emotionally. He had no response. No argument. He was guilty. He'd been sentenced. Now all that was left was for him to do his time. At some point, the mercy train would run out of gas.

"You go see if you can find the property records and deeds. I'll keep an eye on Dexter until Dom arrives." He turned and strode back into the dining room.

His phone rang.

Stone.

He answered. "What's going on?"

"Ambulance is on the way to us. Mama's having severe stomach pain. Emily will stay with the babies. But me, Bridge, Sissy and Beau are heading to the hospital."

Rhode relayed the situation quickly. "As soon as Dom takes him, I'll be right there."

Rhode wasn't sure he could handle one more thing.

What if the cancer had spread?

What if the killer got his clutches into Teegan?

So many what-ifs.

ELEVEN

Teegan rifled through Lorna's office on the second floor. She had rarely used it and once the elevator had broken down, Lorna had stopped going upstairs altogether. Said no point in it. Then why had Lorna been upstairs the day she'd died and how had she climbed up there? She wasn't decrepit, but she'd have needed a cane or walker for balance.

Sifting through the filing cabinet nearest the maplewood desk, she tried to hurry and find any documents on property that Lorna's father had owned. Property that produced oil. This felt so wrong, as if she were violating Lorna's privacy, but this was all hers now. Or might be. A judge might decide to throw out the will and revert back to the original document.

Who were the beneficiaries? Who would the money have gone to? That person might be their best suspect. It couldn't be Evangeline. Teegan's attacker had clearly been a man, but that didn't mean Evangeline hadn't hired someone to do her evil bidding. For the right price.

Dexter Landoon all but promised he hadn't hurt anyone and, on some level, she believed him. He was fit and in great shape. He could be the jester. But why wear the mask? Why that mask? Why not a bala-clava, which would be more difficult to track? How many jester masks could be out there? Why such a terrifying one at that? Was there meaning behind it or was it something the killer'd had on hand—although who had plastic jester masks on hand besides serial killers and psychos or just big fans of trick or treat?

Finally, in the bottom filing cabinet drawer in the back, Teegan found the folder with all the property information and a deal with an oil company to drill. How had Lorna kept that from everyone but Dexter? She hurried from the office when she heard Rhode.

"Teegan, Dom's gone with Dexter." He stood at the bottom of the staircase, his cheeks pale and his eyes pulsing with concern.

"What's wrong?"

"My mom is in the hospital. Stomach pain. I—we need to go. Is that okay?" he asked.

Marisol was in the hospital? "Of course. Yes." She rushed down the stairs and held up the file. "I have this. Dexter was telling the truth—at least about this." But right now that didn't matter. All that mattered was Rhode's mother and her health.

In the car, Rhode white-knuckled the steering wheel and raked his bottom lip between his teeth repeatedly.

"I'm sure she's going to be okay, Rhode."

Rhode kept his eyes on the road and nodded. "What if the cancer has spread to her stomach? What if...what if this is the end? I've already lost my dad and my sister Paisley. I can't lose my mama. I just can't," he whispered on a shaky breath.

She couldn't back up her claim that Marisol would be okay. The truth was she had no idea. She could pray for mercy and hope for the best, but nothing was a sure thing. No guarantees in this life. Silently, she prayed for Marisol and the family, and specifically for Rhode. This kind of stress was the same kind that had sent her mom spiraling into the drink. Seemed like Rhode had had more than his fair share of pressure squeezed on him and this was yet another massive hit.

Lights came into view from behind, blinding her. "Ugh. Don't drivers know to turn off their brights?"

"You'd think, but we are on country roads and it's hard to see deer. I'm more irritated they're on my behind. Step off already," he muttered and increased his speed.

"Should we be—" Teegan's words died on her lips as a vehicle rammed them from behind. Yeah, they should be worried.

Rhode held steady as they lurched in their

seats. Teegan once again silently prayed for their safety. The vehicle rammed them again and Rhode lost all control and careened into a ditch.

The jarring reverberated through her bones and even her teeth rattled on impact. "Rhode?" she said and winced at the pain radiating through her body.

"Yep," he said through a grunt. "You okay?"

"Not really."

The lights zoomed past, an engine revved and then faded into the distance.

"He's gone." Rhode rotated his shoulders, wincing again.

"You say that like you're disappointed." Teegan's muscles spasmed and her hands trembled as the aftershock dissipated and her brain processed what had transpired. They could have been killed.

"I'm not disappointed. I'm confused. Why run us down and not finish what you start? Why not come on down here and put a few bullets in us?" Rhode pinched the bridge of his nose.

"Who cares? I'm glad he didn't. Maybe he thought our crash would kill us. I feel dead." Teegan rubbed her neck, which had bunched and tightened. She was going to be in a world of pain come morning.

Rhode backed up but he couldn't drive out of the ditch. It was too steep. He punched the wheel and the horn gave a weak beep. "I don't have time for this!" Digging out his phone, he pressed Stone's name and, on the second ring, his brother's voice came through the line. Deep and baritone. A little menacing. Like Stone.

"Where are you?" he barked. "They took Mama back. We're all here in the ER waiting."

"We got run off the road. I'm out on Highway 4 and can't make it out of the ditch. I'm going to call a tow truck. I'm sorry."

"No. Don't be. Are you two hurt? Do we need to come?" Stone asked.

"No. The driver ran us into the ditch and kept driving. Don't you find that odd?"

"I do. But let's thank the Good Lord for

the grace and we can discuss ideas later. You sure you don't need me?"

Rhode sighed. "No. He's gone and, if he does come back, I have my gun. I need to call the towing company. I just wanted you to know why I'm not already there. It's out of my control." He grimaced and muttered, "Like everything else in my life right now."

Teegan inwardly flinched. The added stress was her fault.

"Well, the babies are fine," Stone said. "They were asleep when the hullabaloo went down. Don't worry about them."

"Good to know." Rhode ended the call. "Guess you heard all that. Stone's voice carries."

"I did."

Rhode called the towing company and, when he disconnected, leaned his head back against the headrest. "Be thirty minutes." His words were tight. Every minute here was a minute that slipped away at the hospital.

"I'm so sorry, Rhode. All this added pressure on you is because of me. If you want to drop the case, I can find another PI or just trust the cops to do their jobs. Maybe I could take the kids and go somewhere." Even as she said the words, she knew they meant nothing. Teegan didn't have the finances to up and run off with her babies. Lorna's assets were frozen and that meant Teegan was too. She wasn't even accruing new income. Maybe she should again consider returning the excess toys to the stores. The children didn't need them. The splurge had been more about Teegan's meager past than the babies' needs. It might give her a little extra to stretch.

Rhode rubbed his eyes with the heels of his hands. "Teegan, you can stay with us until the contesting of the will is lifted. You said so yourself that the attorney doesn't see the judge throwing it out. It's going to take time, and if the Landoons can push it faster, they will. In the meantime, one of them is threatening you."

"You mean trying to kill me." She had a shallow stab wound to prove it.

Rhode shifted in his seat, his face scrunching at the movement. She was already feeling stiff and sore in her neck.

"About that. I think one of them is threatening you to push you to give up the estate or to forfeit the will, giving it to them. But I think someone else in the family wants you dead. It's not enough to scare you. He—or she—doesn't believe you'll ever scare badly enough to give up a fortune and they aren't taking their chances on a judge."

Two family members. "That's why you're confused about the vehicle running us off the road but not shooting us or something."

"It also explains the damage and threatening notes—warnings to scare you. But then, someone else with a jester mask and a really big knife wants to end things permanently. And I don't know which family member is which or if they're all in on it together somehow. They have a unified cause—getting you gone and their greedy paws on that money and property."

Teegan quivered and ran her hands along the tops of her thighs. "I know this is going to sound shallow, but I can't let whoever is doing this ruin Christmas for me and the babies. This will be the first one where they can open gifts and actually enjoy it. Last year they were confused and ate the paper. Granted, River might eat the paper still but..." She smiled. Her kids could bring her joy even in this nightmare. "Obviously our safety—their safety—is the utmost importance, and I know they don't have a clue when Christmas falls or the true meaning of it, but I guess..."

"You're the little girl who was disappointed each Christmas. You're giving yourself what you never had," he murmured. "You deserve a special Christmas. Every Christmas should be special, Teegan. I want you to have that. And we'll do everything we can to make it happen."

Why was Rhode showing her such compassion and grace? Maybe she should show him the same understanding and kindness. Give him the benefit of the doubt.

But the moment the thought came, a dreaded darkness flooded her mind and heart. Sad memories washed over her.

Mom had been sober for a month and the house had been clean, they'd had food in the fridge and she'd even baked cookies. Misty had turned her nose up and stayed in her room.

"Don't get used to this, Teegan," she'd said. "It won't last. It never does. Stop hoping. It only ends with you locked in the bathroom sobbing and thinking it's your fault. It's not. It's never your fault or mine. So, no, I don't want a cookie. I don't want any sweet hope. Because that cookie won't last and neither will the sweetness." She'd slammed her door shut again and Teegan had eaten cookies and milk with Mom. They'd laughed and watched old movies— where her love for them and theater began. Everything had been picture-perfect.

The next morning, Mom had passed out on the couch with an empty bottle of Wild Turkey, the cookie platter as empty as Teegan's heart.

Rhode rubbed his eyes and groaned. He was still sore from the crash on Saturday.

That night had been a blur. After the tow truck had arrived and given them a ride to the hospital, Mama had been taken for tests and, hours later, they'd declared she had no cancer in her stomach and the pains were likely side effects from the chemo, which was a relief and also grievous. Mama was hurting and there was nothing they could do to change that except some pain pills she hated taking due to grogginess and fuzzy brain. While she lived, she wanted every moment to be lucid. The first thing she'd asked was how the babies were doing and could they get her home to them.

River and Brook were her saving grace.

And Rhode's.

They'd all stayed home on Sunday. Sore, exhausted and frazzled, they'd watched church online and taken it pretty easy, sticking close to Mama.

Moving like Frankenstein, he padded to the kitchen. The house was extra quiet for a Monday morning, and the sky was still dark with a small hint of gray light poking through.

Tomorrow was Christmas Eve and Teegan would be homeless until the court ruled on the will. He'd asked her to stay at the ranch—welcomed it—but she was hesitant. Probably from guilt. His nose drew him to the coffee maker. No one would be up this early except Stone.

"Hey," Stone said as he walked inside from the back porch with Rhode's Labs at his side. Rhode scratched their ears. He'd been gone more than usual and these guys were all about the love, pushing on him and poking their noses under his hands for rubs and licks.

"Hey."

Stone had clearly had a cup or two already. He wore sweats and a hoodie and his stubble had turned into more of a beard. "Everyone's still sleeping. It's been a rough weekend."

As if he needed to tell Rhode. "You think Mama will be okay?"

"Praying so. But there's no guarantee. She's tough and a fighter." Stone sipped his coffee. He was the realist of the family, but they needed that level head. "How's Teegan?"

"I haven't seen her yet this morning but based on how I still feel, I'm going to go with sore and miserable."

Stone smirked. "I meant in general. With everything looming and having to be out of the house. She agree to come here? It's the safest move for her."

Rhode sighed and poured a cup of hot caffeine. He sipped and savored it. "I think she feels guilty for accepting our kindness. Now that she knows about my alcoholism."

"I'm sorry about that."

"She needed to know. Ripping off the Band-Aid was probably best. I'm not sure I'd have ever told her, for fear. She isn't sure she wants the children in my life. She's lived with an alcoholic parent and is afraid. Thing is, I don't hold her fear against her. I'm scared too. What if I do mess up? What if in four years, I don't flee temptation and fall off the sobriety wagon? I can't crush my family again and definitely not my own children. Maybe it's best if I'm at a distance—whatever that might look like. It might be the safer choice for everyone."

Stone poured another cup of coffee and then leaned on the counter, his green eyes piercing Rhode's. "You're aware of the problem. You have a support system. As always, we're going to be with you every step of the way. At some point, you have to live your life, Rhode. You can't exist in limbo. You can't base every choice on whether or not you might succumb at some time in the future. That's not healthy. And it's a sure-fire way to end up back on the drink. Because there's no hope in that."

Stone was right. It killed him that his children might not know him. And if he was being honest, it hurt knowing Teegan might not want to know him better either. Because he wanted her to. He wanted to know her even more as well. He already admired her stamina and strength. He loved the way she loved their babies, and his heart broke at her shattered childhood. A loving and attentive family that got in each other's business too often and could be annoying had raised Rhode, but they were loyal to one another and, at the end of the day, had each other's backs. Their growing-up years had been built on a solid foundation.

Teegan's had been shaky at best.

"You may be right, Stone. But Teegan will not see it that way. I have no idea how to win her trust. I mean I have her trust today. She doesn't trust me for tomorrow or the next day though. Her fears have swallowed up her future too."

"Then maybe just live each day for today. Isn't that what Jesus said? Each day has enough trouble of its own, so don't be worrying about tomorrow's trouble? In twenty-four hours, you'll be upon it. Then you can fight it when it comes. You're a fighter, Rhode. But more importantly, Jesus is a fighter and a finisher of our faith. And if He's fighting for you, you can make it. You can overcome each day and each temptation."

Rhode trusted God to help him each day and, some days, minute by minute. "I know you're right. I just don't know if Teegan will believe so."

"Well, she's a believer. So God will talk to her. Trust that He'll work things out. He's a rewarder of those who believe."

"Thanks." Stirring caught their attention and Teegan entered the kitchen, moving as stiffly as Rhode had been.

"Morning," Stone said. "You need some ibuprofen?"

"I just took some. But thanks."

Stone turned to Rhode. "Until you get your vehicle back, feel free to use the family truck. And, Teegan, the door is open for you. You're welcome to stay here with the kiddos as long as you want or need to. We love 'em. And it's been so good for Mama to have vitality running through the house again. Another generation of Spencers wreaking havoc in the ranch. Sounds about right." He grinned and patted her shoulder before leaving them alone in the kitchen.

Rhode pointed to the coffeepot. "Help

yourself. Won't help the stiffness but it won't hurt either."

She nodded and poured a cup into a Christmas mug. She wore leggings and an oversize sweatshirt with reindeer and stars. Her thick wool socks were Christmas-themed as well. She wore a messy bun that worked for her but shadowy half-moons hung below her eyes. "What do you have planned today?" he asked.

"Stay alive, find the person or people who want me dead, and maybe find our next clue."

The clue. He'd forgotten she'd found it in the tunnel below the estate.

"Did you hear anything new about Dexter from Dom?" she asked, pouring a heaping amount of cream into her coffee.

"They cut him loose. He's technically not trespassing since the estate is frozen right now and, according to him, he was acting in self-defense. Since he didn't actually hurt anyone then there's no crime, but Dom's looking into his history. Seeing if he was anywhere near Addie or her place around the time of her death. And he's looking into where he was the day your sister and Lorna were killed."

Rhode wished they had more concrete news and a better lead, but for now they had nothing. Peter Landoon had dated Addie, which connected to Teegan since she and Addie had been good friends in high school. But it stopped there. He was their solid suspect and, so far, Dom hadn't found a decent alibi.

Teegan put her mug on the counter. "I guess we wait. And I also guess we stay here. I feel torn about that. I don't mean to use you—"

"You're not. But I do want to be in my children's lives. I don't plan to ever touch alcohol again and, let's say I never do... Then what? My children have been spared my presence on the chance I might fail, but if I never do, then everyone has lost. Either way, it's a no-win situation to not be able to have them in my life." He silently prayed she'd see the truth.

She nodded. "You're right. They need a

father and you're clearly a good one. If you never touch it again but they don't know you, it's a fail. And if they do know you and you fall away…it's an even greater pain. I have to decide which is a lesser evil, so to speak, in their lives. I'm struggling, Rhode. To be perfectly honest."

"I know." Now was not the time to push. Only God could change her heart and mind. Pushing for what he wanted would only drive her away. "So what's the clue?"

"Let me get it from my purse." She grunted as she stood and hobbled to the counter, pulling out a tube similar to the one they'd found at the bottom of the swimming pool. She opened it and read, "'My life is a maze of mistakes, but I don't mind, honey. I found you at the end.'"

"Maze. The labyrinth?"

She nodded. "I actually know this one. It's from Lorna's 1963 film with Rock Hudson. *Once Upon a Mistake*. She said she had the maze built because of the mistakes in her life she'd made. Life was a set of paths. If you chose the right path, it would lead to the garden of life. That's why she had an English garden planted outside the labyrinth. But I wonder if this movie didn't somewhat inspire that. It was a few years after she made this film that she gave her life to the Lord and her entire world and purpose changed."

"You want to add searching the labyrinth to our checklist today while we still have the time to be on the property?" he asked. Beau was heading up the investigation and Dom was working it through the law enforcement channels. He had the time.

"Yeah. I also have a meeting at Lorna's law office. Scott returned my call and left a voice mail late last night. We have a court date for the day after New Year's."

"That's fast."

"Not like criminal law. That's what he said anyway. But, yeah, let's see what we can find."

His phone buzzed with a text from Beau and he read it. "Hey, Teeg. Do you know an Olivia Wheaton?"

Teegan paused and nodded. "Yeah. She

was at the reading of the will, remember? Lorna gave her two million dollars. She's the estate manager. I helped her get the job, since we were friends in high school. Why?" Her face paled.

"Because they found her dead in her apartment an hour ago."

TWELVE

Teegan's brain wouldn't process Rhode's words. Olivia was dead? "I don't understand." After the initial text, Rhode had called Beau for more information.

Rhode helped ease her into the kitchen chair. "Just breathe."

She nodded and inhaled deeply, but her chest ached. "How? When?"

Rhode pulled the other kitchen chair around and straddled it, then held her clammy hands. "Beau said her cat was wandering the hallway and a neighbor going out for a morning jog saw her. She tried to take her back. The door was cracked and she found Olivia."

Teegan's chest tightened. "Was she stabbed?"

"Multiple times, and bluebonnets were

left at the scene, like Misty and Addie. The police and forensic team are there now. Stone just texted. We've been called in to clean the scene. I'll need to help my brothers, but Emily has the day off and she's going to be on protective duty. She's tough, capable, and shoots better than any of us Spencer boys."

He meant to lighten the heavy atmosphere and bring her comfort, but the fact she needed protection and that Emily might have to gun someone down on her behalf turned the coffee in her stomach.

"What can you tell me about Olivia? You'll have to tell this all to Dom. He'll want to interview you, so get ready for recounting the statement multiple times." Rhode waited while she swallowed and balled her hands at her sides.

"We went to school together. Her, Addie and me were tight. Practically inseparable. After high school graduation, Olivia went off to college at A&M. She got married after she finished school and they lived in Waco, but about six months ago, she went through a divorce and she moved back to Austin. We reconnected and since she had experience being an estate manager, I got her a job onsite. It's good money. Lorna pays—paid—well, and she and Lorna got along like a dream. She moved to Cedar Springs, so it'd be less of a commute."

"Children?" Rhode's brow furrowed.

"No. They never had children. That was part of the problem, I think. He didn't want them and she did. She thought he'd change his mind. He didn't." Teegan covered her face and the dam of tears burst. Had Teegan unknowingly put her in the crosshairs of a killer? She'd never forgive herself for that. "I don't understand. Why her? Why Addie?"

"I don't know why her. Addie had a connection to Peter Landoon. Olivia, too, just by working here, but do you know if they might have had a personal relationship?"

He rubbed her upper shoulder but nothing brought comfort at the moment.

She shook her head. "I know Charlie had taken an interest in her. He'd asked her to dinner a couple of times, but she wasn't ready to date yet. She was still grieving her marriage."

"How did Charlie take it? Did she say?" Rhode asked.

"He understood. Charlie went through a divorce two years ago. She said he was sympathetic and they were on good terms. Which is surprising because he's skeezy to me. But then, she needed a friend and sometimes our need…" She trailed off as it dawned she was no different than Olivia. Sometimes a person's need blinded them to truth, deceived them.

Was her need to protect the children from Rhode based on her own pain blinding her?

"Take your time." Rhode sipped his coffee. "We can connect the women to two Landoon men personally. And, who knows, maybe Peter can be connected to her and you didn't know. He's at least seen her on the property. They all have. But why kill her unless they're so greedy they wanted the two million too?"

Teegan wiped her tears and peered up at

Rhode. Turmoil swam in his ebony eyes and she could tell he was keeping something from her. "What is it? What aren't you saying?"

"Nothing. I don't want to scare you. I'm just thinking."

Understatement of the century. "I'm already afraid, Rhode."

"You're the center. You own everything. You were friends with Addie. Addie dated Peter. You got Olivia a job and you were friends with her. Misty was your sister. They all died in the same manner. Only Lorna's death was different. Something else is going on here. I wish I knew what. It's like I can taste it but can't pinpoint the flavor."

"Tastes metallic to me." Like blood.

"We should know more later. Do you want to be alone?"

Yes. No. The sound of babies crying drew her attention.

"I'm happy to take baby duty and feed them if you want to lie down."

"Actually, the babies will soothe me.

Their joy is contagious and, right now, I'm pretty low on joy. Even if it's the time of year that brings great joy." She stood and Rhode followed her to her room. The twins were already standing in the crib they'd been sharing. The room wasn't exactly spacious, but it was cozy and comfortable.

"Ma-ma. Ma-ma!" Both babies reached out with huge grins. Not any idea that evil lurked right under their noses. They had no cares and simply trusted Mama would take care of them. They were safe. Loved. Knew they'd be provided for.

Childlike faith.

Right now, Teegan's faith was a bit wobbly. She lifted Brook from the crib and Rhode reached for River. He went right to him as if deep within he knew Rhode was his father.

"Hey, little man. Did you sleep good?" Rhode asked and kissed his little cheek then frowned. "Wow that diaper is heavy." He glanced at Teegan. "When do babies potty train?"

"Depends on the baby. I think I could actually train Brook now. But, River…well you just have to change the rivers flowing in his Pampers."

Rhode chuckled and snagged a diaper then laid River on one side of the bed while Teegan took to changing Brook on the other. Once they were in fresh diapers, they all headed for the kitchen. River repeating "juice" over and over.

"We're gonna getcha some juice, bud." Rhode rubbed River's dark hair and when he wiggled for freedom, Rhode put him down and Teegan let Brook loose. They chased after Rhode's Labs and the good sports seemed to enjoy the game of tag.

"If I could bottle that baby energy, I'd be the richest man in the universe," Rhode mused.

"Right?" Teegan said with a smile.

"How about I make pancakes?" Rhode asked. "Do they like pancakes?"

Teegan laughed. "Yes, but it's going to take an army to clean the syrup out of their hair and anywhere else."

"Hey, if your food isn't sticky and messy,

what's the fun in eating it?" He went to the pantry and retrieved a griddle. "I could always put maple syrup in the batter to make them sweet already."

"Will that work?"

"Will that work?" he asked as if her skepticism was ridiculous. "I don't know. I've never done it." He laughed and Teegan's knotted neck relaxed at the breath of fresh air. The joking and normalcy of making breakfast was what she needed to battle the unsurmountable fear and dread.

As Rhode worked at making pancake batter and adding a heaping amount of maple syrup to it, she kept an eye on the kids. The toys his family had purchased kept them occupied and River had a special love for Rhode's oldest Lab. He leaned against the furry friend while crashing trucks against one another.

Teegan made them juice cups and enjoyed how much the children felt at home, as if they'd always come to the ranch, had sleepovers here. Belonged. And if truth be told, Teegan felt a part of the family too. Other than Lorna's hospitality, Teegan hadn't felt so welcomed by anyone else.

Bridge entered through the back door into the kitchen. "Pancakes. Score!"

Rhode pointed a finger at him. "I didn't remember inviting you to breakfast, bro. Besides, pancakes are carbs. Don't want to ruin that nice figure," he teased.

The Spencer men were fit but Bridge had taken it to a whole new level. His guns bulged through his Henley, but he wasn't like bodybuilder big. Just seriously dedicated to weights. "Har har. Where's the kiddos?" he called loud enough for them to hear. "I have presents. Maybe toys!"

As if they understood, they came toddling into the kitchen. "How did my brother father such cute kids? I hope you have your mommy's brains or you're done for." Bridge baby-talked and laid two gift bags on the table then scooped up a twin in each very big, very strong, arm.

"You want a present?" he asked them.

Brook nodded and River pulled at his short beard.

Rhode snorted. "I'll have you know my mind is sharp and could outmatch you any day."

"You wish. Stick to pancakes." Bridge sat the kids on the table and handed them each a little red gift bag. River pulled out the white tissue paper and shoved it in his mouth. "Aw, you take after your dad after all," Bridge teased and removed the paper from his mouth and wadded it up. He was a natural with children. Teegan wondered why he wasn't settled and a father himself. He helped River look into the bag and her son removed the little Dallas Cowboys nerf football. Navy, silver and white.

Brook was already tossing the tissue paper out. She, too, had a Dallas Cowboys football. In pink.

Bridge grinned. "Equal opportunity here."

Teegan snickered. "Thank you."

The kids attempted to clamber off the table and Bridge scooped them up and set them down, and off they went throwing footballs and giggling and talking gibberish that they seemed understand. She and

Misty had had a language only they could interpret too. Her heart ached for her sister, her friends. Lorna. When last she'd talked to her attorney, he'd informed her that they were holding a graveside funeral tomorrow morning. Family only.

Teegan wasn't even able to say a final goodbye to Lorna and it ripped out her heart. Her only solace was knowing that Lorna wasn't really in the cemetery but in Heaven and one day Teegan would see her again. Once the service was over, she'd go pay her respects privately and leave flowers.

Rhode plated several pancakes and handed one to Teegan. "It worked."

She bit it into it, tasting the sweet maple flavor. "No-stick pancakes. You're brilliant."

"Teegan, you're the first person on the planet to call my brother brilliant," Bridge said. "That doesn't really speak well of you." He shoved an entire pancake in his mouth and winked at her. Oh, this man was a character. The whole family was fun.

Emily padded into the kitchen. "Morning. She held up River's football. You forgot to teach him how to yell 'incoming' before he throws." She rubbed her head. "He's got good aim. I'll teach him to shoot in the spring."

Teegan laughed at her dry humor. Bridge shoved Emily playfully as she poured her cup of coffee.

"Hey, easy. You don't want me to spill a drop of this go-juice. I need it."

After she poured in a large helping of cream and sugar, Rhode snorted, "You want some coffee with that cream and sugar?"

"You want to live five more minutes? Target someone else." Emily made a dramatic display of taking that first delicious drink.

After feeding the babies—and an easy cleanup thanks to Rhode's pancake ingenuity—they dressed them for the day.

Rhode and Bridge grabbed their coats and Rhode hung back. "I'll be a phone call away if you need anything. Emily will keep you safe."

"You two seem close."

"Well, we weren't always." He glanced at Emily playing catch with the babies, smiled with fondness, then followed Bridge to the crime scene.

To Olivia's crime scene. This couldn't be real.

She plopped on the floor next to the fiery redhead and mindlessly played ball with the children. Emily tossed the pink football into Brook's lap. "Hey, Rhode will make sure to keep you and the babies safe. We all will. I know how hard it is to trust though."

"Yeah. How do you know?"

"Because I was a target of high-profile people during an investigation that included the late eldest Spencer sister, Paisley. Working for the Public Integrity Unit—well…the fact there has to be a PIU says it all. And I'd just found out my father had a whole separate family for my entire life. To say I had trust issues is an understatement. But Stone was patient with me. Like Rhode's patient with you." She leaned back and grabbed the ball River had tossed, missing.

"Rhode said y'all got off on the wrong foot."

"I cut his legs out from him, actually. I let his alcoholism shape my thoughts concerning him. He was friends with our suspects—yes, plural—and I let his past cloud my judgment. I thought he was either involved in the murders or tipping off his buddies with investigative information. We had some serious verbal blows. In the end, I was wrong. And he showed me grace. He also showed me a lot of ice. But I deserved it."

They sat quietly.

"He's a God-fearing man who stumbled in a really big way and it robbed him of everything he held dear." Emily chucked the ball again further to make River run for it.

"I'm scared he might slip again."

"No one is more afraid of that than Rhode, Teegan. And you can't measure him with the yardstick of fear. That's not fair." Emily's soft brown eyes met hers. "He loves these babies and if I had to guess... he loves you too."

"No. We're not a couple. It was just a one-night thing that humiliates me to this day."

"Because you made a grave mistake and got drunk. God forgave you. He forgave Rhode too. Maybe it's your turn."

Maybe Emily was right. But how did she overcome this fear and dread?

The scene from earlier had been as gruesome as the first site where they'd cleaned up the blood from Misty and Lorna's deaths. Olivia Wheaton had at least put up a fight. Based on the setting, Rhode surmised she'd opened the door to someone she'd known. No forced entry. She'd let her killer inside. Then it had taken a dark turn. After the few hours of cleaning, he'd been wiped out, but there was no rest for the weary.

Mama had called to tell him that the Christmas festival was happening downtown tonight and that they wanted to take the babies. That Teegan had already agreed.

Rhode had called Teegan to arrange to meet her at the Landoon estate to find the next clue and then to go with her to the meeting at Lorna's attorney's office. He'd also mentioned grabbing a bite of dinner and meeting the family at the Cedar Springs Christmas Festival.

She'd agreed to that too. Was she softening up to the idea of him as part of the twins' lives? Or...part of hers? How did he feel about that? Up to now, his heart had been set on being a father but he couldn't deny that Teegan rang all the bells in his heart. But he had nothing to contribute, especially if the court decided to keep the will as it was. Then came the biggest hurdle. Would she wholly trust him? Because if she had any inkling that the shoe would drop and he'd fall off the wagon, he could not, would not, be with her. How was he supposed to be with someone who didn't trust him?

But then, did he fully trust himself? In this moment, yes. His sobriety was such a gray area.

He pulled in behind Teegan's car, Bridge's Pilot and a sleek black SUV. Who else was at the estate? Bridge must have come to protect Teegan, but the other vehicle...

His stomach knotted and then jumped to his throat as he bounded out of the vehicle with his gun pulled. The front door opened and Beau and Bridge walked out with a hulk of man he recognized as Axel Spears. Beside him, the bodyguard who had been assigned to Beau's sister, Coco, after her attack had put her in a temporary coma. Since she'd awakened, she'd been doing great and was now heavily involved in their church. It was nice to see his childhood friends serving the Lord.

Libby Winters, the lady bodyguard, approached with bright blue eyes and a dark ponytail bobbing. "Mr. Spencer," she said and reached out her hand for a firm handshake. He reluctantly accepted it.

What was going on?

Axel Spears, former FBI, extended his massive paw. And Bridge thought *he* was buff? This guy blocked the sun. He and his silent partner, former CIA operative Archer Crow, ran Spears & Bow bodyguard and security services international. But why were they here? His confusion must have been obvious.

"We've been hired as added security. Here is a photo of Amber Rathbone, our other female team member who may assist."

Early to mid-thirties with dark eyes and hair.

"And your other male colleague?" Would Archer Crow be watching over Teegan?

Axel and Libby exchanged a knowing smirk. "He sticks to the background, but even if he was on duty—you'd never know it. He's known for being a phantom."

Rhode let it go. "I don't understand. Did Teegan hire you?" Not that he was against added protection. His ego wasn't so large that he felt intimidated. The more safeguards the better, but they weren't cheap. At all. Only someone with Beau's... "Beau hired you."

Axel nodded once. "He did." He exchanged another smirk, this time with Bridge, as if they knew each other well.

"Do y'all know each other?" Rhode asked. Bridge never mentioned it.

"From our FBI days," Bridge said.

That was it? Seemed like more to him. "I assume Teegan knows."

Axel nodded and ran his hand through coal-black hair. Darker than even Rhode's, it was almost blue it was so black, but it had a few pops of premature silver. "Libby will be on the house with the babies just for precaution. We don't feel they're in direct danger. But we don't want to underestimate this guy. We've talked with Miss Albright and she's given us all the information she can, and Beau has updated us on the case."

Bridge slapped Axel on the back in a friendly gesture. "We'll talk soon. I need to get going."

"Yeah, we will. I want a yes next time I see you."

Bridge shook his head and smirked. "I know you do. No one ever said you weren't persistent." He slid behind the wheel and Rhode frowned.

"Been trying to get your brother to come

work for us. Part-time if he wants to keep working for the aftermath recovery." Axel sighed. "You have any questions?"

About a million. Bridge leaving the business? How long had Axel been asking him? A lot of what Bridge did in the FBI was classified and, from what he could tell, Axel's work might have been too.

"No. Not right now. We have phones and you'll be wherever we are. That works."

They shook hands again and the bodyguards swaggered to their trucks. He remembered that kind of confidence but his had been shattered when he'd wrecked his career. He was building it all back though. A career and the confidence.

He heard Libby Winters laugh and turned. She shoved Axel into the truck. "Shut up," she teased. She must have some serious power packed into that petite frame to budge Axel. If body-guarding didn't work out, the World Wrestling Federation would hire him.

Rhode entered the house. Teegan met him

in the entry, eyes wild, and gnawing on her bottom lip. "I need expensive bodyguards!"

He had a sneaky suspicion she would be more alarmed by added protection than the comfort of security. "It's Beau's way of helping me out more than it is to scare you. He thinks I'm worried I'm not enough." He kicked at the marble floor. "Maybe I'm not." At least, not in her eyes.

Teegan licked her lips. "You remember that verse in the Bible where the man said I believe but help my unbelief? That's how I feel about you. I trust you. And I don't. I hate that. And it's about me, not you. Which sounds so cliché, but it's true. I have to work through what's springing out of me. My fear. My doubt. My projection onto you. I don't know how long that will take."

"I appreciate the honesty." He swallowed the lump in his throat and exhaled. "Okay, let's find a clue."

"Right. 'My life is a maze of mistakes, but I don't mind, honey. I found you at the end.' Let's head to the labyrinth."

He followed her outside, the wind whipped and the temperature had dramatically dropped in the past couple of days. It was in the mid-fifties, which for Texas was cold. He wore a navy sweater with a navy-and-white-checked dress shirt underneath and jeans and a brown leather coat. Teegan wore a pair of faded jeans and a cardigan over a T-shirt. She shivered.

"You want to go back inside and grab a jacket?" he asked.

"No."

He shrugged out of his coat. "Hold up."

She paused and he moved into her personal space, encircling her with his arms as he draped the jacket over her shoulders and she slipped her arms inside the sleeves. He held the collar of the coat with his hands and searched her eyes, hoping to find unadulterated trust.

"It's warm," she said.

"I generate a lot of body heat," he said.

She swallowed hard. "I think maybe I remember that."

He arched an eyebrow. He'd had some

of his hazy memories surface in the past week too.

"I remember this smell. Leather and something…like…sandalwood maybe. Just you, I guess," she murmured.

He brushed a windblown strand of hair from her eye. "Maybe." He held her gaze a moment more, the air swirling with tension—the good kind. The kind that turned into kisses and, if not controlled, something far more unbridled. He dropped his hands and his gaze. "Lead the way," he said, purposefully ending the intense moment.

She nodded and turned on her heel, guiding him expertly through the maze. Wind rustled in the boxwoods and the sky was painted muddy gray.

"I hope it doesn't rain out the festival tonight. Sounds fun."

"It does. I couldn't say no. I love Christmas festivals and parades. Your mom seemed excited. I hope her strength holds up so she can go."

"Me too." His mom's cancer always loomed like a dark shadow in his mind.

No one was getting out of this world alive, but he wanted more time for her and with her. Wanted her to see his babies grow up. Wanted them to know and remember her.

But life didn't always work out perfectly. Rarely did it. He hoped anyway.

At the end of the labyrinth, Teegan paused. "I think it will be here, since she said 'at the end.' I'm just not sure if it's the very end, so let's start on each side and work our way forward to the very end of the labyrinth. And we can't forget it could be buried under concrete or something. You never knew with Lorna."

He was finding that out. Rhode dug into the thick boxwoods, pushing into the gnarled branches and feeling around. "The tops are often trimmed, so I think if she tucked a clue into the hedges, it would be the middle or the bottom to avoid being found before she wanted someone to, or being destroyed with hedge trimmers."

Teegan was already on her hands and knees working her way up in a grid. He mimicked her on the other side. They spent the next thirty minutes switching from comfortable silence to small talk. Teegan shared baby stories, including her pregnancy and the hardships of carrying twins.

"I wish I could have been there to help you through it."

"I know. I would have told you but…"

But they'd had no idea who each other was or how to find one another.

"Hey. Wait a minute! There's something… I can barely feel it. My arms aren't long enough."

Rhode crawled over and reached his arm inside, feeling her fingertips against his, and his pulse spiked. "It's like a hard case."

"Yes," Teegan said, her eyes wide and full of excitement.

Pushing further into the hedges, he clasped the small case and maneuvered it through the branches until he pulled the box free. He handed it to Teegan. "You open it. She wanted you to."

Teegan smiled and opened the tiny safe that was clearly weatherproof but not locked. She pulled out a tube like the others and unrolled the paper. How many more clues did Lorna have on the property?

"'All that I have, I give to you, darling. Two wrongs don't make a right, but you in my life is anything but wrong. You have my whole heart. You're buried deep within me and I will always love you.'" Teegan low hummed. "I think I know the movie, but the location is a blank."

"What movie?"

"*Mr. Right*. From the late fifties. She starred opposite Cary Grant again. I think this movie may have been inspiration for using mostly right turns to get through the labyrinth."

Rhode scrunched his nose. "You don't think it's somehow going to be buried with her, do you?"

"Ew. No." Teegan's face softened and a tear sprang in her eye. "Sorry, it's just I wasn't even invited to her funeral, and all I have of Misty is ashes in a small urn."

Teegan had had little time to grieve her sister or Lorna. He couldn't imagine. "I wish it wasn't that way, and I wish you had some time to process, but even now…time is short. We have to head to the attorney's office, then dinner and the festival."

"I know." She blew a heavy breath. "As far as the movie line, I'll chew on it. This one is tough. I believe she intended it that way. But she must have trusted that I could figure it out."

"You will."

Rhode only hoped they'd stay alive long enough to do exactly that. This killer wasn't going to give up.

THIRTEEN

Teegan fidgeted as they entered the imposing brick attorney's office in downtown Austin. Inside the lobby, an ostentatious Christmas tree at least thirty feet tall twinkled with soft white lights. Rhode pressed the elevator button and the doors opened. They rode it to the tenth floor. Leave it to Lorna to hire sharks. But then, she'd known what she was up against. Her own family had smelled the blood in the water.

The halls were abuzz with attorneys flitting around with papers and cups of coffee. Reception pointed them to Scott Carmichael's office, and he welcomed them inside. Teegan glanced around the clutter and disorder. Not exactly what she'd been expecting.

"Have a seat, Teegan." He swept his hand

out. "And Mr. Spencer. Sorry about the mess. I haven't finished unpacking and making this my own. It used to belong to James DeVoe. He died in a tragic accident a couple of months ago. Did you know him?" Scott pushed a few boxes away and then took a seat.

"No. Lorna might have. Usually she saw Sylvia."

Scott smiled as he rifled through a drawer, retrieving an ink pen. "I've only been with the firm about a month, but I assure you I have read up on the case and am prepped."

"I believe you."

Scott went through the case in great detail and explained the law in the style of *Law for Dummies*. He took statements from her, and jotted everything down. He noted all the attacks and Rhode's theories about two Landoons trying to kill her: One through scare tactics and the other with a knife.

Scott's eyes widened with each new attack Rhode relayed. "I'm sorry. Do you have any evidence this has been done at the hands of the Landoon family? Anything I can concretely bring the judge?"

"All circumstantial," Rhode said.

Scott nodded and made another note. "I'll contact Detective DeMarco and have him send me police reports." He closed his notebook and smiled, a lopsided sweet smile with perfectly straight teeth. He'd had braces. No one's teeth could be that perfect, and it reminded Teegan of her imperfections and the lack of funds she'd had to right them. "Teegan, you have a strong case and I don't see the court throwing out the will. Anything else that might help me?"

"In full disclosure—if it comes up at the hearing," Rhode said. "We have reason to believe Lorna also buried a treasure of sorts on her property. Nothing was mentioned in your reading, but I wondered if she had any notes about it with instructions for you to remain silent."

Scott's eyebrows raised. "She didn't mention she had a treasure, but I've heard the rumors since I was a kid. I grew up nearby and I'm pretty sure it's been national news—well, tabloid national news."

Teegan had seen it in tabloids before too. "We've found clues. That personal letter was about treasure."

"Well, if you find it before the will's decided, you won't be able to spend it or keep it. Maybe slow your search down." He winked.

Not a terrible idea.

"Who did the estate go to prior to the changes?" Rhode asked.

Who had the most to lose was his real question.

Scott flipped through a mountain of papers in a thick file and his lips twisted to the side. "Evangeline and Dexter received the lion's share then the rest was split equally between the grandchildren and great-grandchildren. Harry Doyle was given sole ownership of the thoroughbred business, including all thoroughbreds. Nothing is in here about Teegan or the estate manager, Olivia Wheaton. But this was written before either was in her employment."

Whoa. That was a massive change. And if she wanted Harry to stay on because he was a good man, then why take him out of owning the business, and give it to Teegan? That was odd. Unless Lorna felt Charlie or another Landoon could swindle Harry out of it, but not Teegan.

But if Harry knew this, he'd never mentioned it. Could Harry have motive? He could be connected with Olivia but not Addie. He had no reason to kill either of them.

Rhode dipped his chin. "That's what we needed to know. Thank you for your time."

They shook hands and left his office, bumping into Sylvia Bondurant, who had handled most all of Lorna's private things. "Mrs. Bondurant, how are you?"

"I'm well." She glanced toward Scott's office. "How is the case going? I heard the will had been contested. I'd have been more surprised if it hadn't been. All of Lorna's family members are piranhas and always have been. Her biggest regret."

"He's doing a great job. When she rewrote

her will, you were present. She wasn't under duress."

"No. She was sharp and bright, and I plan to testify to that." She nodded resolutely. "It's hard not being on the case but we thought it best since I needed to be a witness. Scott taking over made sense. He's new and unbiased. Teegan, she wanted you to have it, and she trusted you to steward it well. She thought of you as family." Her smile was tight. "I have to run. Good to see you. Kiss the babies for me." She bolted down the hall.

As they left the building, Teegan frowned. "I'm surprised Lorna didn't leave anything to Sylvia. Not that you have to leave money to your attorney, but Sylvia has worked with her for over a decade and bent over backward for her, showing up whenever Lorna called and catering to her every whim. Seems like she'd show her some appreciation monetarily. If I win the case, I'm going to see she receives a gift. She deserves it."

Rhode opened the passenger door for her and she slid inside. "You're a generous person, Teegan, and she knew you wouldn't be stingy." He jogged around the front of the vehicle then slipped behind the wheel. "We're running late. Festival is underway. You want to eat there? I'm sure they'll have vendors and all sorts of food."

"That sounds good." But she was miles away in thought.

"Hey, are you okay?"

"I don't know. I have this nagging feeling. Like I should know something that I don't." She popped her knuckles. A habit she thought she'd kicked.

"You've had a lot happen and you've had no time, like you said, to grieve or process. It's like when you're rushed to get out the door but you feel like you left something behind. Once things slow down, you won't feel that level of anxiety."

He was probably right. "I guess." But she wasn't sure.

While Rhode drove, Teegan ruminated on the meeting and who might be behind all of this.

They parked in a public lot in downtown

Cedar Springs. The streets were lined with cars and people wandered in droves to all the shops, which had been festively decorated. The air was frosty and carried scents of pine, cinnamon and barbecue. Her stomach rumbled as she inhaled the tangy smell.

A food court had been set up in one section and was congested with food trucks and vendors selling cookies, hot chocolate and other baked goods.

"You see the fam?" Rhode asked.

The fam. He had made her a part without batting an eye. Not *his* family. Just the fam. She could use family right now. She was basically orphaned. "I don't."

Rhode pulled out his phone. "I'll text Stone."

"You see the Spears & Bow peeps?" she asked, darting her gaze among the throngs of people chattering, laughing, and kids romping and shrieking with excitement.

"No, but if they don't want to be seen, they won't be. Axel all but said that." Rhode's phone beeped and he read his message. "Mama is moving slow. They're still about twenty minutes out. Let's find food and we'll meet them in line for Santa in twenty."

"Perfect. I'm starving."

After pushing their way through the crowds, they stood in line for barbecue sandwiches piled with pulled pork and topped with tangy sauce. Rhode had slaw on his but she was not a fan of slaw. She squeezed ketchup onto her hand-cut fries and dug in. "This is so good."

Rhode nodded through a full mouth and handed her a napkin. She dabbed at the sauce spilling onto her chin. No one said barbecue wasn't messy. They perched at a picnic table and ate their dinner while watching the festivities and listening to the live band sing Christmas songs. At the moment, the lead was crooning "Holly Jolly Christmas" in Michael Bublé fashion.

When they were finished eating, Rhode threw away their trash and they strode for the other side of downtown where Santa sat in a wonderland nestled into a Christmas tree lot, complete with fake snow. Teegan paused at a tent full of Christmas quilts and holiday-themed pillow covers. "These are beautiful," she commented. The price tag was too big for her—at least, with her limited funds and Lorna's assets frozen.

Rhode nodded and they strode on.

"Hey, there."

Teegan recognized the voice and turned with a grin. Harry Doyle stood with his hands in his pockets. Harry was like a beach after a storm. Completely disheveled and weathered from years outdoors. He smelled faintly of hay and leather.

"Harry. What are you doing here?"

"Needed a little breather. My son is meeting me here in a few minutes. Tradition."

Harry was always big on traditions. Teegan admired that. She wanted to start traditions with her own children. Maybe the festival would be their first.

"I'm so sorry about Olivia," he said. "She was a good person."

"She was."

"I heard about the will. Charlie came by the stables an hour or so ago. Told me what was going on. I still have my job, but I'm sorry about yours."

"Well, it's not over yet," Rhode said. "Teegan will be back in the house after Christmas."

Harry's eyebrows raised. "The Landoons have always gotten what they wanted. I wouldn't hold my breath. I hope I'm wrong, though, of course." He waved a hand as if it was nothing, but his expression was grim and he'd yet to make full eye contact with her.

Teegan clenched her teeth and forced a smile. "Of course." Harry had always been a nice man, but it seemed like he wasn't rooting for her to win. Or maybe she was simply paranoid, and with every right.

As they headed for the Santa line, Rhode glanced back. "Was his behavior odd to you?"

"Yes, actually. What is that about?"

"I don't know. Probably nothing. Stress. And he's hunting for his son, so he wasn't paying much attention. Didn't the attorney say he was on the docket to testify on Lorna's behalf?"

Teegan nodded. "Harry saw Lorna every single day without fail. They were friends."

"Did he have access to the house?"

"Of course. Lorna trusted him." She studied his wary eyes. "What are you thinking?"

"I'm not sure. But he seems to be pitting his money against you. And that raises my suspicion. I wonder if he's been bribed somehow. With the horses or money or both. We should, at the very least, tell Mr. Carmichael our suspicions. The last thing we need is him getting caught unaware if Harry plans to perjure himself."

Teegan agreed and then heard, "Ma-Ma!" She turned as the Spencer family came into view. Beau and Sissy let the twins down and they rushed to Rhode and Teegan. They each scooped up a baby and Teegan watched as Rhode's face brightened. She knew that look. The same one she had each time she saw them.

Pure joy and unconditional love.

She took in his family. Marisol with her cane for support. Stone and Emily, Beau and Sissy and Bridge. That was what family should look like. It nearly brought her to tears the way they loved the babies and her.

"I never realized how hard is to wrangle two small children who can't even outrun me." Stone grinned. "I was half tempted to rope 'em like calves."

Teegan laughed at his teasing.

"They are slippery," Bridge said. "It was like watching him try to capture greased pigs in a 4-H contest. I have video." He held out his phone.

"You do not," Stone protested. "I told you not to video me!"

"Oh, but I did." Bridge waggled his eyebrows and pressed Play. Teegan and Rhode watched as Stone tried to chase down the babies to put on their shoes. A pink football flew and pegged him in the head.

"Bridge! I have enough to deal with here," Stone griped. "I'd rather wrangle killers. It's easier. Is it wrong to cuff a kid?" he muttered.

Teegan snorted. He was going to make a great dad. The enjoyment in his eyes overrode his complaining.

"It's baby shoes, bro. You've lost your edge," Bridge said.

"You better not be videoing me, Bridge." A football pelted Bridge in the head, causing the camera to shake.

"Okay. Okay!" Then the video ended.

Stone shook his head but chuckled. Emily tucked her arm into his and beamed.

Yep, Teegan would say kids of their own were in the near future.

"I'm going to take Mama over to the benches so she can watch. No point standing in this line for eternity when you can have a front-seat view," Bridge said.

Marisol kissed Teegan's cheek. "You get used to the rowdiness and picking. Teasing is our way of lovin'."

"I see that." And she loved it. "Can I bring you a hot drink? Cider, hot chocolate, tea or coffee?"

"No, dear. I'm happy to sit and see my grandbabies squirm on Santa's lap. The boys have taken a poll on if they'll cry or not."

Teegan laughed again. "They don't meet strangers."

"Just so you know," Sissy said, "I voted they wouldn't cry, but River would pull off Santa's beard."

That was more likely than tears. "Good call." They'd know soon enough.

Well, Sissy won the poll. River had successfully ripped away Santa's beard while he'd worked to keep Brook from removing his glasses and destroying them. Rhode had wondered if it had been a planned blitz attack from his little minions. Mama had loved every second and remarked how much they reminded her of him and Sissy at that age.

After the Santa debacle, they'd all eaten cookies and listened to the live music before taking the babies to see the reindeer and to make reindeer food, which consisted of oats, edible glitter and a carrot. The extremes parents went to in order to make

Christmas special was beyond him. The greatest miracle of Christmas was Jesus Himself.

But Rhode was all on board with helping the kiddos scatter the food on the ground, knowing the wind would blow it all away, and he'd probably even take a few bites from the carrot to prove Rudolph had had his snack. Like his dad used to eat one of the cookies, take a bite out of the second and drink all the milk. The first thing Rhode had always done on Christmas morning was race to see if Santa had eaten the cookies and drunk the milk. Then Dad would read them the Christmas story from the Bible before a free-for-all broke loose on the gifts.

Once they returned to the ranch, the babies were wiped out and whiny. Teegan put them down, wanting some time alone, and Rhode was now discussing the case with his brothers and Beau.

"Any news on Kenny Lee?"

"Same knife that killed Misty, Addie and Olivia was used on Kenny. So he's been ruled out as the murderer," Beau said. "If I had to guess, I'd say he stalked Misty here and got in the killer's way. He then disposed of Kenny's body. I'm not sure why though. Why not leave him dead in the house?"

"Maybe he thought he could hide him and frame him. Any blood evidence could be assumed Misty had hurt him during the attack. No body meant he could be on the loose and doing this." This made the most sense to Rhode.

Stone and Bridge agreed.

Teegan entered the living room. Rhode's old and gray dogs ambled up for petting. "Sweet ole boys." She rubbed their heads.

"I don't like to think of them as old. Just wise. Old means their time is growing short and they've been my best friends for so long—"

"Because humans don't like you," Stone teased.

Teegan chuckled.

"Anyway," he stressed, ignoring his brother's smart remark, "I can't bear to lose 'em."

"You'll have to bury 'em with our other gone-but-not-forgotten friends," Bridge said somberly.

"Death is hard no matter animal or human." Teegan sighed. "So, were y'all discussing my case?"

"We were," Rhode said. "Is there anything about Addie and Olivia you can tell us that might be important?" The two women had connections to the Landoons. Rhode could buy that Peter may have killed Addie as a jilted boyfriend. But why kill Olivia unless she'd seen or heard something she wasn't supposed to?

Charlie was still on the table too. Could he have done something that Olivia had witnessed or said something she'd overheard?

"Nothing that would cause their murders."

"Were they close with Misty?" Rhode asked.

"Misty was hard to get close to. She was guarded, and could be tough to deal with at times."

"Meaning?" Rhode leaned his elbows on his knees.

"She was the Regina George of our school." Teegan darted her glance around the room. Rhode's eyes narrowed. And, based on his brothers equally confused expressions, they were lost too.

"Know my crowd. I forget not everyone is a movie buff like me. Regina George is a character in the movie *Mean Girls*. She was *the* mean girl and her friends— loosely called friends—were loyal out of fear of consequences. They hung out with her and went along with her nastiness. Sort of like Olivia and Addie with Misty. They cheered together. Neither had a real mean streak. Misty…could be mischievous in a dark way. I hate even talking ill of her. She had way more good parts."

"I'm sure she did," Rhode said.

"Well, if that's all, I'm going to try and sleep." A divot formed along Teegan's brow, revealing the same expression from earlier at the festival.

Rhode excused himself and followed her

down the hall to the guestroom. "Hey. You still feel like you can't make a thought or memory surface?"

"Yes. How did you know?"

"I'm getting pretty good at reading you."

"Part of your job and all," she said.

"No. I mean yes, it is, but no. I just... I just like to know what you're thinking and feeling." He inched closer and inhaled her sweet scent. "If I'm being honest. But I haven't forgotten we're just friends. We are that, aren't we?"

She held his gaze. "Absolutely."

"Good. And the feeling you're having?"

She squinted and shook her head. "It's like a memory rose from the depths. It's hovering just underneath the surface. Unsettling, but important. I can't make it bob above the water and reveal itself. But, again, the past few days have been a blur. A million things going on, being said. It might be nothing."

"Try to sleep. That always helps me. You want me to bring you some spearmint tea? Mama says it always helps her rest."

She touched his arm. "No. But thank you. I appreciate your thoughtfulness." Teegan slipped into her bedroom and closed the door with a quiet click.

Why did he feel like he'd lost something he never had?

FOURTEEN

Teegan flew up from a fitful sleep, sweat pooling in the hollow of her throat and on the back of her neck, hair sticking to her skin. She couldn't remember her dream, but it was important. Ugh. What was it? What had she remembered subconsciously?

She couldn't bring it to the forefront, but she did know where to find the next clue. She checked the clock on her cell phone. Almost 4:00 a.m. Now was the time to do the search, before light broke through the sky and the estate became a hustle and bustle with people, which meant eyes. And where they were going would stand out to anyone. Plus, she only had four hours to be out of the house. It was Christmas Eve.

After quickly brushing her teeth and changing into sweats and a hoodie, she tiptoed to Rhode, who was sleeping on the couch with his laptop on his chest. She appreciated his commitment to find the killer. And somewhere out there one of the Spears & Bow bodyguards kept watch.

He reminded her of River, the way he snoozed. His hair fell in his eyes and stubble covered his normally baby-smooth face. One man should not be this attractive. Surely, other women must think the same thing. No matter, he was stupid good-looking to her. Not to mention, patient and kind and funny.

"Rhode," she whispered as she shook him.

His eyes quickly opened, revealing he'd only been dozing. "I know where the next clue or treasure is. I know what the attorney said, but I want to go anyway. Just to see if I'm right. We have to go now though. And…and we'll need shovels."

Rhode sat up ramrod. "Shovels? What time is it?"

"Four. It'll take a bit of time and I'd like to do it before dawn and the babies wake, but someone needs to know we're gone in case they wake early. I don't have much time before I'm thrust off the estate."

Rubbing the scruff on his chin, he nodded. "Give me five minutes, and I'm going to text Libby and let her know we're going out onto the property so she doesn't shoot if she spots us. I have a feeling she's a 'shoot first and ask questions later' kind of woman."

Teegan smirked. "Yeah, she seems tough."

Rhode padded to the bathroom with his black duffel bag. When he returned, he smelled of mint and he'd changed into jeans, a violet Henley and a flannel shirt with the same color mixed in. "Okay, Emily has the baby monitor. Let's go dig it up. Where are we going? You haven't actually said yet."

"A cemetery."

Rhode did a double-take. "A what?"

Teegan grinned, excitement building. This could be it. The treasure. "Now you know why I left you in suspense. Come on. I'll explain when we get there."

After arriving at the estate, they headed to the gardener's shed. "The clue was, 'All that I have, I give to you, darling. Two wrongs don't make a right, but you in my life is anything but wrong. You have my whole heart. You're buried deep within me and I will always love you.'"

"How does that play into a before-dawn dig in a cemetery?" Rhode asked. "Don't you already think we're living a horror movie? You now want to add a creepy cemetery? I'm already freaked out." Rhode hunched against the early morning wind, his flashlight poking out of his sleeve; he'd pulled his hands into them.

"That's fair, but last night you talked about not wanting to discuss the fact your dogs are getting old and Bridge mentioned burying them. The only thing Lorna loved more than her children were her two greyhounds, Chaplin and Claudette—after Charlie Chaplin and Claudette Colbert. They were her pride and joy and, when they passed, she buried them on the backside of the property. Headstones and all.

They're buried deep within her, but also in the ground. They had her whole heart. I'm ninety-seven-percent sure it's there."

"That or we're pulling a Randy Travis for nothing."

Teegan snorted and handed him a shovel from the shed. "I'll be singing 'Diggin' up Bones' all the livelong day now. Thanks for that."

Rhode smirked.

Teegan closed the door, her own shovel in hand. "It's out past the English garden near the woods. I didn't see Libby's car. But I know she followed us here."

"It's her job to stay hidden and that includes her vehicle. She'll be doing perimeter sweeps. We should take her coffee after we're done. It's cold and who couldn't use the caffeine?"

"Good idea."

They marched toward the east side of the property and Teegan shivered and paused.

"What's wrong?" Rhode asked.

She wasn't sure but the hairs had raised on her neck. "I feel…watched."

"Might be Libby. Remember, they watch but we can't see them. You probably feel her eyes on you. Who would know we'd be out here this early? I didn't even know."

"Fair enough."

They passed the garden, scents of flowers crawling through the air. Teegan's nose started to run from the cold. Back near the woods, she pointed to the rectangular iron gate. Inside were flowers and a big tree, a bench and two headstones. "Lorna would come out here before she grew too old and visit them. Talk to them. She said it was a peaceful time that she treasured. Another reason I think we've found the right place. She treasured her dogs."

"If I dig those dog bones up and the note says they're the treasure as some kind of Lorna joke, I'm gonna be fit to be tied FYI." Rhode opened the gate and it yawned an eerie, lingering squeak, sending a shiver through Teegan.

"I'll start with Chaplin. You dig up Claudette," she said, and drove her shovel into the hard-packed earth. Her sore muscles from the car crash and being stabbed protested, but she continued. Scoop by scoop, removing soil. "Digging holes to bury a dog—or a body—is a lot of work. There has to be a better way for serial killers to hide their victims."

Rhode paused and studied her, the flashlight beams shining up from the ground, illuminating the amused gleam in his eye. "Really? That's the topic you want to land on?"

She shrugged then kept digging.

"How far would a woman—or someone who hired the gardener—bury a dog? Surely not six feet," Rhode mused. He continued digging, his scoops bigger and faster than hers.

"I don't know. Far enough that another animal wouldn't dig them up. But how far down is that? I'd google it but I forgot my phone in the car."

"Not smart." His lips twisted to the side and he went wide-eyed.

The unsettling sensation returned with a vengeance. "Rhode? What's wrong?"

He patted his back pockets and then his coat pockets and frowned. "My phone must have fallen out." He grunted and picked up his flashlight, scanning the ground for his cell.

Teegan resumed digging and hit something hard. "Hey. I think I found something." She dropped to her knees. "Can you hold that flashlight over me? I can't see."

Rhode stopped hunting for his phone and shined the light over Chaplin's grave. No dog bones, thank the Good Lord, but she spied a black box like the one in the hedges, only bigger. Maybe 8.5 x 11. She hefted it out of the open grave. "A clue."

"Well, don't leave me all alone and in the dark. What is it?"

His words struck her. "What did you say?"

"I was kidding."

"I know." A memory finally bobbed to the surface, clear enough for her to see. "I remember something."

"Go on."

"A dance. Like a Sadie Hawkins dance,

only called the Bluebonnet Dance. I didn't want to ask a boy so I didn't go, but Misty, Olivia and Addie did."

"What happened?" Rhode asked.

"Misty did what Misty was famous for. Being a prankster at someone else's expense. I didn't know about it until it was too late. Misty wouldn't tell me who she'd asked. Said it was a surprise and if I wanted to know to come to the dance. She knew I wouldn't. I would have stopped it. She knew that too."

"Stopped what?"

Teegan leaned on her shovel with one hand and held the dirty box in the other, the memory turning her stomach. "Misty had asked a boy named Anthony—as a joke. Anthony was sweet but he was socially awkward and he had a severe underbite, so some of the bullies called him Moonface. It was horrifying."

"If you didn't go to the dance and she didn't tell you who her date was, how did you find out?" Rhode asked.

"After the dance, Misty called me and

told me a bunch of kids were going treasure hunting on the Landoon estate. Mom
had been asleep for a while and I wanted to
go. So, I locked up any liquor I found and
headed to the estate. Just like I told you."

Rhode frowned. "If Misty was a popular cheerleader and he was a kid who was
bullied, why would he believe she actually
wanted to attend with him?"

Teegan's stomach lurched at that cruel
night. "Because, unbeknownst to me, she
was pretending to be me. I was always nice
to Anthony. We talked about old movies
and books. He was obsessed with the *Lord
of the Rings*. I ate my lunch in the library
and he often did too. Different reasons,
same safe space."

"That was pretty vile of her. Sorry."

"No, you're right. It was."

"What happened at the dance?"

Teegan wasn't completely sure since she
hadn't attended but Addie had confided her
side of the story later. "Addie gave him a
note from me, aka Misty. It told him she
would rather spend the night alone with

him, like we'd spent time alone in the library, and to meet her at nine o'clock at the Landoon estate. They could treasure hunt together and watch the stars."

"He bought it?"

"He had no reason not to. And, Rhode, you have to understand he was socially awkward, a total introvert. Not to mention, he trusted me. This was an introvert's dream! No crowds. No forced dancing or chitchatting with other students who often made fun of you."

Rhode heaved a heavy breath. "I kinda don't want to ask what happened next."

It was tragic. "Misty had clued in some of the football players and other friends. They arrived before nine and hid around the lake, in the boat and in the boathouse. When he sneaked onto the dock where she'd instructed they meet, she'd already laid out bluebonnets and was in the water. She told him to hop in—for skinny-dipping. She'd laid her dress on the dock, too, but she had on a swimsuit."

"He didn't," Rhode said, his eyes wide.

"Why wouldn't he?"

"Go on."

"He stripped down and so many kids jumped out, laughing and heckling. Addie said it was horrific. Misty was in the water, cackling, and said they didn't need the moonlight with his chin. She actually said that. And he thought I had talked to him that way." Teegan wiped away a few tears. "It gets worse."

"How?"

"Because he started crying then jumped in the lake. Addie said they thought he was swimming out to Misty to do something bad, but he didn't surface. Finally, a football player had the sense to realize he was drowning himself! He dove in and brought him out of the water, but he wasn't breathing. He gave him CPR and he came to. No one even called an ambulance, Rhode! He could have died."

"What happened when he woke?"

"By then, most everyone had scattered. He ran off with his clothes, crying. That's when I arrived. I didn't even realize it was

Anthony until Addie and Olivia found me and confessed what Misty had done pretending to be me."

Rhode low whistled. "That is seriously messed up, Teegan. Did you confront Misty?"

"That was the only time in my life I laid hands on her. We came to blows and I shoved her hard into the bedroom closet. We didn't speak for over two weeks. And when I returned home that night, Mom had found a bottle I hadn't and was drunk. I should have stayed home. Misty had wanted me to be there. Wanted me to think it was as funny as she did. Or maybe she'd wanted to be mean to me too. I don't know."

Rhode shook his head. "Did you try to make it right with him later?"

Teegan had wanted to but it had been the last week of school for seniors. "Anthony didn't return to school the following Monday, and he didn't walk with us at graduation. He disappeared."

"Why did you think of it now?"

"Because Addie told me that while he

was on the dock, before he'd seen Misty in the water, he'd said not to leave him alone in the dark. He was scared of the dark. She said they'd snickered at that, but tried to keep it quiet so he wouldn't hear them out there. I guess being out here at night and those words brought it all back. Sadly, I haven't thought about it in years. And we never spoke of it again."

But she was certain Anthony had thought about it often and carried the pain and humiliation with him. She hoped he hadn't let it define him…but the bluebonnets. Misty. Addie. Olivia. She'd been so focused on the Landoon family threatening her, it hadn't crossed her mind this might not have a thing to do with the inheritance left her. But it explained why someone had threatened her to scare her, and why someone else wanted to butcher her and left behind bluebonnets.

Rhode's mind reeled a million miles a minute. The sick tragedy that had happened well over a decade ago and the fact he'd been looking at these attacks all wrong. They needed more information on this Anthony guy. Where did he live now? Work? Had he been in contact with Addie or Olivia—or even Misty? He needed Beau and Dom on it immediately.

"What's this guy's last name, Teegan? Do you remember?"

"Um…" Her eyes grew to the size of balloons and her mouth dropped open.

"What is it?"

"I can't believe it. It's Doyle. Anthony Doyle."

"Doyle as in *Harry* Doyle?" Could this Anthony have been his son or grandson? Harry was in his mid to late sixties, if Rhode had to guess. He'd been weird at the festival and that's when Teegan had had those strange vibes. It was convenient that a gunshot had sounded out at the stables but the attacker hadn't been shot. If Harry was the attacker and heard the sirens, the shot could have been a cover for him. He was helping to protect Teegan. But really, he was the one after her. He was always in the stables according to her but was conveniently missing during the attack.

Harry had been employed by Lorna for years. He would have known about the multiple passages that led to the tunnel. The attacker had disappeared from the wine cellar, but the door had been locked. There must be other ways in and out of the house.

Revenge for a loved one was a strong motivator, and Harry was in great shape.

Snapping of twigs jarred Rhode from the conversation. He placed his finger to his lips and drew his gun. They stood listening to wind rustle the leaves. The noise could be deer or other nighttime critters still creeping around before dawn.

But Rhode's gut warned him it was dangerous. Eyes were on them and they weren't Libby Winters'.

"Stay here. I'm going to check it out."

"Let's just go back to the house," she pleaded.

"If he's out here stalking you, I'm finding him. And if I have to put him in this dog cemetery to keep you safe, I will. Sit tight. I'll be right back."

"Everyone knows no one comes back in a horror movie after saying they'll be right back, Rhode!"

A flock of birds burst from the branches as if spooked.

A predator.

"Rhode," Teegan whispered with urgency. "Maybe we should just—" She screamed and pointed behind him. Rhode spun around in time to be charged by the jester, who knocked his gun from his hand.

Teegan squealed.

The blade came down quick and hard, entering Rhode's gut, but he didn't feel pain. Adrenaline had already kicked in, protecting him to fight or take flight. Then the jester ripped the blade from his flesh and he did feel that.

Searing. Throbbing pain.

Raising the knife again, the jester brought it down and struck his shoulder, shoving him to the ground.

"Run, Teegan! Go!"

When the blade raised again, Rhode grabbed the jester's arm, holding it back. He never saw the sucker punch coming.

Everything faded to black.

The jester raised his face, hidden beneath a terrifying mask, the knife dripping with Rhode's blood. Teegan bolted, dropping the box. She didn't want to leave Rhode, but if she stayed, the jester would kill her too.

Rhode.

Dying in a pet cemetery if he wasn't already dead—he'd hate that. Teegan had to flee and find help. "Libby!" she screamed as fear consumed her and adrenaline boosted her speed as she ate up the ground. But Libby knew Rhode was keeping a watch over Teegan and could be in a sweep a mile away on the other side of the estate.

In the early morning haze and hustle, Teegan had rushed off without her phone and Rhode had lost his. Teegan couldn't fight a killer and try to recover Rhode's phone or gun.

The jester was hot on her heels and gain-ing. Teegan darted toward the lake and the boathouse, hoping to hop in the boat and get as far out on the lake as she could. He'd never make it to the other side on foot before her.

She hollered again for Libby, her voice carrying on the dark wind. Her pulse pounded in her ears, but she kept her eyes locked on the boathouse where they kept the keys.

Behind her, heavy footfalls fell faster, harder, and her blood turned cold.

Moonlight glittered on the water even as the clouds morphed from inky black to slate gray as the sun worked on its approach to dawn. Up ahead, the boathouse came into view. She could make it. But what if Rhode was dead? What if it was too late?

Images of River and Brook kept her rushing forward with all her might. As she reached the boathouse, she glanced behind her. The man in the white mask, bathed in an eerie glow, approached, and her hands fumbled to open the door, but she managed it. On the right hung a pegboard full of keys, one set belonging to the speedboat.

Grabbing the keys, she turned to race to the boat, but the jester—Harry—now blocked her path. Could she appeal to him as a parent? She, too, had kids now. She had to try.

"Harry, please, don't do this."

He slowly cocked his head, his grip tightening on the knife. Ice raced through her veins.

"I just figured out today that it's you. I understand your fury. I do. But you need to know the truth about that night. I've always wanted to tell it to Anthony, but he vanished."

He stood eerily silent, his head still tipped to the side.

She continued. "Misty pretended to be me. I would have never done something so cruel. Please don't do this. I have children and while I know I'd want revenge for their humiliation, killing isn't the answer."

He inched toward her and she shuddered. "Take the mask off, Harry. Let's talk like adults." If she could appeal to any sliver of humanity left in him, she would, but not when he was wearing a mask of wicked confidence. "Please." No last laughs tonight. Just truth. And, hopefully, forgiveness.

Harry reached for his mask and Teegan felt a tiny sliver of relief. He knew her. Knew she wasn't capable of menacing behavior.

Slowly, he pulled the terrifying plastic face from his and Teegan stumbled backward, shock quaking in her veins.

"Not who you expected? Crazy what a jaw reconstruction, working out and a new haircut will do for the appearance."

Scott Carmichael's handsome face stared back at her.

The transformation was astonishing. But the weird nagging she'd felt in his presence now made sense. She'd known him all along but couldn't place him. It wasn't Harry jarring memories, but Scott.

"But your name?" What was happening?

How could he work at a top law office in Austin with a phony name?

"Anthony Scott Doyle. After the terror you and your friends reigned, I was too embarrassed to stay the same person. I changed my last name, taking my mom's maiden name. I went to law school, searching for ways to make you pay legally, but you know what? There's nothing one can do to scum like you for bullying a person almost two decades ago."

"I didn't—"

"Stop lying!" he bellowed, raising the knife. "I'm so sick of lies and pranks. Of people like you. I got the wrong sister the first time, but I'm not sorry."

Actually, he hadn't killed the wrong sister. The irony was terrifying and tragic.

"Misty was nothing but a vicious viper with a pretty face. But you can't pretend, can't get out of this. You knew things I hadn't told anyone."

True. Misty would have had to gain his trust somehow. "She must have overheard us talking in the library. I didn't share our conversations with her." But she had shared them with Olivia and Addie. They must have confided in Misty.

"Liars never stop lying. I was humiliated. For years. And that was just the cherry on top. I couldn't even go to my own graduation for the embarrassment. That's what you and your sick friends did to me!"

Teegan remained silent.

"You ran a long con on me. Made me into the butt of all your jokes. I trusted you, Teegan. Thought you were different. But you aren't. Your kids will be better off without you." He stepped forward and she retreated. "You ran a long con. So, I did too."

"I don't understand."

"For being smart, you're pretty stupid," he said through a sneer.

Where was Libby? Where was any help? She inched her arm behind her back, feeling along the wall for anything that might be handy to use as a weapon. She was cornered like a mouse with a big cat, fangs bared, ready to pounce.

"When Dad told me you'd become the caretaker for Miss Landoon, I set it all in motion. I stopped at the stables a few times. Knew Lorna's attorney. A real shame James DeVoe died, but it made a spot available for a new attorney. Me." His wicked grin revealed that the lawyer's death had not been accidental. Scott had killed him. As far as knowing about the tunnel, he could have always known because of Harry. He'd been employed at the estate for decades. "But I had already been working that angle, schmoozing one of the named partners. So when he died... I was right there with the plans to become Lorna's main attorney, get close—to you. Maybe even get to know you. Pretend to like you. Pretend to be your friend—or more—and betray you too. I knew Sylvia would never give up those billables, so I set another plan in motion, but then Lorna went and fell down the stairs and I found a new way in."

Be unbiased and run the reading of the will. "Why didn't Harry speak to you at the reading of the will? If you're his son."

"Dad knows some of what happened that night—that I'd been embarrassed. He presumed it was because I wasn't a good dancer and awkward around people, and I let him believe it. With the changes to my name and physique, I asked him not to let anyone know we were related, including the Landoons. He always respected my wishes. I suspect because he had a hunch the night of the dance was far worse than I let on."

Teegan's mind reeled. Harry had been cordial but never overly friendly. "He fired a warning shot at you! He could have killed you. His own son. He'd have never gotten over that."

"There's always risks involved. It was worth it."

If he was willing to let his father almost kill him, then why hadn't Scott copped to killing Lorna? "You act as though you didn't murder my employer. An innocent woman!" She continued searching for a weapon, but nothing.

Scott made another move toward her. She was trapped inside the boathouse. Only one exit that he was blocking. "I didn't kill Lorna. I'd decided you weren't worth the game, the seduction. It was time for you to die. When I arrived, she was already at the bottom of the stairs and your sister was standing over her. I assumed you'd killed her for the cash. Which wasn't surprising. But I guess your sister did it or maybe the guy who'd been there with her."

No way. Misty would never! She had no reason to kill Lorna—or anyone. Teegan didn't believe him.

"Kenny Lee?"

"Don't know or care. He saw me and was running for the car. I couldn't let him get away and I knew Charlie was on the property. I used the golf cart and dumped him in the woods."

Wait. If Kenny Lee was running for Misty's vehicle, then he must have been with her. They must have gotten back together. Or there would have been two vehicles. But Teegan would never fully know. Kenny and Misty were gone.

Finally, her hand grasped something slender and wooden. An oar! She gripped it and kept to the shadows, waiting for the right moment to strike and praying Libby would come this way to do a perimeter check.

"Did Harry keep you in the know? Is that why Lorna cut him out of the second will? Had she overhead something and that's why you killed her? Because my sister would never have done that."

Scott laughed and her blood curdled. "After what you say she did to me, you don't think she'd shove an old lady down the stairs? Either you didn't know her at all or you're lying about your involvement that night of the dance. Bluebonnets were a nice clue, but you never put it together. You wrote me off. Forgot about it all. But I never forgot. I've remembered it every day of my life."

"I—" She had forgotten. Instead she said, "I'm sorry. And I'm sorry if it cost your dad the business. Your heartache and grief. I am sorry." And she was. None of that should have happened.

"Dad didn't want the stupid business. Too

much headache. When Lorna told him she'd willed it all to him, he asked her to amend it to keep him with a clause he couldn't be let go, but he never wanted the headache of owning a business. He wasn't about the money—not like her family."

That actually made sense. Two feet. That's all she needed and then she could use the oar to clobber him and escape to the boat.

"You were going to actually be my lawyer in court?" Part of that long con.

"No. I never planned to go to court. You're going to be dead. It won't matter. Talk time is up." He rushed her and she thrust the oar out, knocking him off balance; the knife clattered to the dock. She raced for the boat, keys in hand, and ready to speed to safety, call the cops and ambulance, and free them from this nightmare.

Scott's hand latched onto her shoulder and she screamed.

Gunshots rang out. One. Two.

Scott's hand released and she turned as he fell to the dock in a crumpled, dead heap.

Libby!

Teegan snapped her attention toward the figure on the dock. Not Libby.

Rhode!

His body was bent forward, one hand holding his stomach. His purple Henley was darker in the middle now from the blood. In the other hand, he held his gun.

"Rhode!"

"It's over," he rasped and collapsed on the dock with a thunderous crash.

Teegan's heart stopped and she froze for a second before launching herself in his direction. She dropped to her knees in a pool of blood. "Rhode! Rhode!"

But he was unresponsive.

She could not lose him. The babies couldn't lose him. She'd been such an idiot. "Rhode, please stay with me. I… I love you. I need you. We need you." She brushed her lips to his clammy brow. "Please don't die. Please live."

"Let's just chalk this up to God's perfect timing, which pretty much seems to be later than we want," a woman's voice remarked with utter calmness and even a hint of humor. "I found blood at the pet cemetery and then heard you scream."

Libby emerged from the shadows, her light conversation as if no one had nearly died or was dying. But then she spotted Rhode and her expression sobered and she darted into action, checking Rhode's pulse. "He's alive. Apply pressure." Libby guided Teegan's hands to Rhode's abdomen then checked Scott's pulse. "He's not." Two bullet wounds side by side filled his forehead. One from Rhode. The other from Libby.

Teegan couldn't control her tears as she peered down at Rhode. Helpless. Lifeless. He'd risked it all to protect her. "I can't lose this man. I love him."

Libby's face contorted, pain unmasked. "Sometimes the people we love most...they don't always make it."

FIFTEEN

Teegan tiptoed into Rhode's hospital room. After the police and EMTs arrived at the Landoon estate, Rhode had been rushed into surgery. Thankfully, he would fully recover from the injuries and would be allowed home the day after Christmas. Best gift ever. Teegan had been stuck at the police department, going over her statements for what felt like hours, and all she wanted was to kiss her babies and be at the hospital for Rhode. Libby had sat with her the entire time, which was not in her job description, but it meant the world to Teegan to have her support and her help in filling in the gaps.

Libby had foregone using the golf cart because it hadn't blended into the shadows like patrolling on foot. Lorna's property was so vast, when she'd heard the faint scream, she'd come running. Libby could run a six-minute mile. Impressive.

Teegan's friend Yolanda had picked up the children so the Spencer family could all be with Rhode. She'd taken them to her parents' home for some Christmas Eve festivities. It was now nearing evening, the day had been long, exhausting, and not exactly full of the Christmas spirit.

Rhode slept peacefully. She ran her finger through his hair, so thankful he'd been spared.

"Hey," she said.

Rhode's dark lashes fluttered and then his eyes opened. He studied her face and smiled. "Hey."

"How you feel?"

"Like I was stabbed in the shoulder and the gut, but it's all good." He shifted on the bed and winced, but in true Rhode Spencer form, he had his wits about him—and his wit.

"Can I get you anything?"

He patted the bed and she eased beside

him. "Stone and Bridge are in the waiting area. Sissy and Beau went to pick up food, and Emily's now at the ranch with your mom."

"Is Mama okay? I know I probably set her back."

"She's fine. A strong woman who raised a strong family. Dom was here too."

"What did he say? About the case? Is it really over?" Rhode asked.

Teegan nodded. "He questioned Charlie after I told him Scott denied killing Lorna. It fit. No knife. But Charlie lawyered up fast. They brought in Evangeline and pitted the two against each other. When Evangeline heard she'd be tried for the murder, she started talking. According to her, Charlie sneaked onto the estate because he'd overheard Harry on the phone with Scott about asking Lorna to take him out of the will as inheriting the business. That she'd done it. Charlie knew the will had been amended and wanted to see it himself."

"And Lorna?"

"That wily woman saw him, got suspicious, and had the audacity to climb those stairs and confront him. It turned into an argument and, according to Evangeline, Charlie shoved her and she fell, but it was an accident. He panicked and left, calling his mother and telling her what had happened. She instructed him to stay silent. So she's in trouble but not as much as Charlie."

"And the other threats like painting your car and running us off the road?"

"All Evangeline and Charlie to scare me, as you thought. They hoped it would cause me to give up."

"Was Harry involved?" Rhode asked and cleared his throat. "Can I have a drink?"

"Of course." She poured him a cup of water and helped him sip.

"Thanks. So, Harry?"

"Harry didn't know the real story about Anthony's past at the estate or that he was the one killing people. He said the name change was to sound more like a prominent attorney. And, to be honest, I think that's somewhat true." She relayed everything Anthony, aka Scott, had told her on the dock. "I think Scott mostly wanted to be someone else. He hated the boy who was picked on and all he represented, and Harry did know about him being bullied in general. So he agreed to all the changes and wishes of secrecy." Teegan brushed a bang behind his ear. "This was all a revenge plot."

"Not exactly," Rhode said. "Beau came by a little earlier. They found items in Scott's house. Photos and trophies."

"Like serial killer trophies?"

Rhode nodded. "During Scott's college years, two girls were stabbed and bluebonnets left near the scene. But it wasn't multiple stabs."

Teegan covered her mouth with her hands. "You're kidding."

"That's not all. While Scott clerked for a judge in Dallas, one of the paralegals also died by a stab wound and bluebonnets were left behind. So, I don't think it was just revenge. I believe Anthony Doyle, aka Scott Carmichael, was a serial killer and used revenge to kill more women, including attempting to murder you. I think the revenge was how he personally targeted you, Addie and Olivia."

A serial killer? Had that night broken him so badly he'd grown an urge to kill? No. He'd had a choice to make. He could have overcome his past. Teegan had. Instead, he'd chosen to make heinous choices. What was done to him had been vicious and wrong, but everything he'd chosen to do was on him.

"What about the VICAP? I thought it would have let you know about similar murders."

"Sometimes law enforcers get behind on paperwork and entering information into the system. If it's not entered into the database, it's not there to find. Who knows, there might even be a larger trail of murders in the places Scott lived and worked."

Teegan sat stunned, her hand still in Rhode's. She had so much she wanted to say. So much to apologize for.

"I do have some good news—other than I'll live."

She chuckled. "What's that? I could use some good news."

"Dom said in light of the circumstances, you get the estate. No court date. It's yours. No moving into the ranch, and you can do whatever you want for the babies."

Tears sprang to her eyes. Christmas in their home. The only home the babies knew. But that paled in light of what she wanted to say. "I have good news too."

"Yeah?"

She wiped her eyes and laid a hand on his cheek. "I love you."

His eyes widened and shined with moisture. "You do?"

"When you dropped on that dock, I thought you were dead. And, in that instant, I realized I wanted you in our lives. Completely. Not me as your accuser but as your support system. Our children need you. Not any dad. You. God is going to help us walk this journey out and I want it to be together. If I haven't hurt you so badly you don't want to try."

Cupping her neck, Rhode gently drew

her to his mouth. When his lips met hers, he whispered, "This is the best Christmas gift ever. I love you, too, Teeg. So much." Then he kissed her with such tenderness and care, she almost cried again. This man was not perfect. He had a past. A dark past. But the enemy did enough accusing and guilt-tripping of his own. She was not going to add to it. She would be his biggest champion, right next to Jesus.

When he broke the kiss, he grinned. "Sorry I ruined Christmas. I know you had all these grand ideas. Nothing went your way."

True. "I've learned Christmas doesn't have to be perfect by what I do or buy or when I put up a tree. It's not about a day. It's about who."

Rhode's mischievous eyes sent a flutter through her. "You're not going to go all 'Jesus is the reason for the season' greeting card on me, are you?"

She laughed. "No. But it's true."

"It is." He kissed her hand. "I want you to know that I don't want your money and you can never think I would be after it because I don't have much. So I'm fully onboard with a prenup."

Teegan snorted and started to bring a witty comeback but then his words dawned and her heart galloped in her chest. "Rhode, you said prenup."

His grin turned wily. "Well, yeah. I'm going to marry you. Duh."

She couldn't contain the joy bubbling all through her. "Well, I'm gonna say yes. Duh. And I don't want a prenup. If we're together it's til death do us part, and all that I have is yours too. Lorna would want it that way."

"I guess that's settled then." He kissed her again.

Teegan broke away. "We can't spend Christmas Eve making out in a hospital bed."

"Why not?" His tone was innocent but teasing filled his dark eyes. "Then what will we do?"

Teegan removed a thick envelope from her handbag. "Open it."

Rhode did as he was told and perused the stack of papers. "It's a screenplay."

"Lorna's treasure we found in the pet cemetery. I had Libby retrieve it after all the chaos. It's a screenplay she cowrote with one of Hollywood's most famous directors—Charles Kendrick. A Christmas screenplay!"

"Wow. This will be worth a lot of money." Rhode low whistled. "What are you going to do with it?"

"I think Lorna wanted me to find it because of my love for theater and movies. We had that in common. I can't say it would have ever seen the light of day had I not come along."

"But you did. And I have a feeling I know what you're going to say."

"What's that?"

"You're going to go back to the local theater and pitch this play and perform it. Next Christmas, if I had to guess."

Teegan's eyes pooled again. This man truly knew her. And so had Lorna. She would represent her and her hard work well.

"That's exactly what I want to do. What Lorna would have wanted."

"Lorna knew you would treasure it and do the right thing, not try to sell it and make a fortune, like her kids would have. Lorna's legacy will live on, through you. Can't beat that kind of treasure." Rhode ran a hand over the old typed pages. "Can we force Bridge and Stone to be Christmas carolers?"

"I thought you wanted to help her legacy not hurt it."

Rhode chuckled. "You are amazing. I can't wait for you to be my wife."

She leaned down and kissed him again. "So you know, my calendar is wide open."

* * * * *

If you enjoyed this
Texas Crime Scene Cleaners story
by Jessica R. Patch,
pick up the previous books
in this miniseries.

Crime Scene Conspiracy
Cold Case Target

Available now from
Love Inspired Suspense!

Dear Reader,

Like Rhode, you might battle an addiction. You may have fought some battles and lost some too. God is gracious. He's the giver of millions of chances. He's with you in it all and I hope you could relate to Rhode and to the sweetness of God to take what spiraled into a nightmare into something beautiful. For those of you who might live in fear like Teegan, God is able to handle your fear and your future. Walk in grace.

I'd love for you to be part of the Patched In community through my monthly newsletter, where you can receive a short thriller for free when you sign up at www.jessicarpatch.com, and visit me on Facebook. We have so much fun there!

Warmly,
Jessica R. Patch